# That Scatterbrain
# BOOKY

## BERNICE THURMAN HUNTER

**Scholastic Canada Ltd.**
Toronto New York London Auckland Sydney
Mexico City New Delhi Hong Kong Buenos Aires

**Scholastic Canada Ltd.**
604 King Street West, Toronto, Ontario M5V 1E1, Canada

**Scholastic Inc.**
557 Broadway, New York, NY 10012, USA

**Scholastic Australia Pty Limited**
PO Box 579, Gosford, NSW 2250, Australia

**Scholastic New Zealand Limited**
Private Bag 94407, Greenmount, Auckland, New Zealand

**Scholastic Children's Books**
Euston House, 24 Eversholt Street, London NW1 1DB, UK

Grateful acknowledgment is made to the author for the photographs on pages 4, 40, 174,
188, 313, 317, 338, 369, 436, 468, and 483; to the Eaton's Archives for the photographs
on pages 38, 46-47, 63, 67, 95, 200 and 244; to the James Collection, City of Toronto
Archives, for the photographs on pages 75, 118-119 and 150-151; to the Canadian
National Exhibition Archives for the photograph on page 142; and to the Globe and Mail
for permission to reprint the article from the July 15, 1936 Globe on page 302. Photo on
page 334 by Gordon Wyatt. The author acknowledges the use of "Be Good, Sweet Maid,"
from "A Farewell" by Charles Kingsley.


Cover photographs by Steve Wilkie courtesy Shaftesbury Films.

**Library and Archives Canada Cataloguing in Publication**
Hunter, Bernice Thurman
That scatterbrain Booky / Bernice Thurman Hunter.
ISBN 978-0-545-98618-2
1. Depressions--1929--Canada--Juvenile fiction.  I. Title.
PS8565.U577T48 2009      jC813'.54      C2008-905182-3

ISBN-10 0-545-98618-7

*To Mum and Dad*
*who loved me*

# Contents

# 1

# A note from school

Skinny legs flying, I ran straight home from school. My mum was in the kitchen starting supper.

I asked the same old question. "Where's Dad?"

She gave the same old answer. "Out looking for work."

It was September, 1932, the heart of the Depression.

I handed her the note the school nurse had given me and ran lickety-split up the stairs to the bathroom.

When I came back down (with my dress caught in my bloomers), I knew something was wrong because Mum wasn't paying much attention to the note. I already knew what was in it. I had sneaked a look on the way home from school. *Beatrice is twenty-two pounds underweight,* said Miss Malloy's sterile handwriting. *We recommend that you contact your relief authorities. Any Canadian child exceeding the twenty-pound underweight limit is eligible for free government milk.*

Ordinarily this information would have upset my mum to no end. But today she just plucked my dress out of my bloomers and remarked absently, "You'll have to eat up, Booky."

I already ate up everything in sight, so that didn't mean much. But her calling me Booky did. It meant she wasn't mad at me and I wasn't going to get heck for anything. And it meant she loved me. That funny little nickname told me so.

My mum was a pretty woman. She had dark wavy hair, high olive cheekbones, and big brown eyes that flashed when she was mad and sparkled when she was glad. Today they were circled with blue and tired looking.

Her stocky five-foot frame was too well rounded for her liking. "I only weighed ninety pounds on my wedding day," she'd regularly sigh. But in spite of that she was a very good looking woman.

In her flat little size-three house shoes she was barely two inches taller than me. Standing on tiptoe, I kissed her ruddy cheek. She gave me a fierce hug that cracked my skinny bones.

That was my mum.

"Change your dress, Booky," she said, slivers of potato peelings flying from her paring knife.

"Okay, Mum."

I wasn't always so obedient, but when my mother called me Booky (she pronounced the first part Boo, like Boo-hoo) I'd jump off the roof for her. I ran back upstairs two at a time.

My sister Willa wasn't home yet. She was the oldest and in high school. She had a long walk home. My brother Arthur was next. And then me. His school bag was on the table, so I knew he had been in and gone out again. He was lucky. He never had to stay in for arithmetic. That's what had kept me late, arithmetic.

In my old play dress and holey running shoes I made a bee-line for the back door. Rummaging under the rickety porch steps I found my hoop and stick, and controlling it expertly, I flew like the wind up the street to Audrey's. Not once did my hoop wobble or fall over and have to be started again.

Audrey Westover was my best friend. She was adopted. That meant her parents could afford her. They picked her out on purpose. When I first found that out I ran all the way home to ask my mum if I was adopted too. I hoped I was because that would mean Arthur wasn't really my brother. Mum greeted the question with a big hoot of laughter. "Go on with you, Bea," she chided good-naturedly. "It's easy enough for me to get children without going out looking for them."

Now that was my chance to ask something I'd always wanted to know—how people go about getting children—but just then the lady from next door came over to borrow an onion and the thought went clean out of my head.

I could hardly believe the difference between the Westovers' house and ours. Ours, the one we were living in now, was a skinny, stuck-together row house. The uneven floors, upstairs and down, were covered with cracked linoleum, splotched brown where the pattern had worn off. Naked light bulbs dangled on frayed black wires from tattered, papered ceilings, and we didn't own such a thing as a house lamp. All our furniture was old second-hand stuff.

Outside, the house hadn't seen a lick of paint in years. Both front and back porches were made of peeling, rotted wood with broken steps and unsafe, worm-eaten railings.

Behind the house stretched a narrow weed-patch yard, enclosed by a high dilapidated board fence. We never managed to stay in one place long enough to have a flower bed or to grow grass from seed. Mum said that was her heart's desire, to stay put long enough to have a perennial bed across the front and a vegetable garden in the back.

But one thing redeemed our house. Inside, it was the cleanest house in the world. Our old furniture gleamed with lemon oil. Hawe's floor wax shone on the patternless linoleum, and the air fairly tingled with vinegar and Lysol. I'll bet anything you could have eaten your supper right off our kitchen floor without getting so much as one germ in your mouth.

By comparison, the Westovers' house was a miniature mansion: a fashionable bungalow situated at the far end of Lilac Street. It had a cement front porch with a wrought-iron railing, and it was all hemmed in with grass and shrubs and flowers.

Inside, it was so filled with carpets and furniture and lamps and things that it gave me a peculiar, crowded feeling. But the biggest difference, the one I noticed the most, was on their supper table. (Except that at Audrey's, supper was called dinner and dinner was called lunch. To me, lunch was brown-sugar sandwiches in a paper bag.) The Westovers' supper table was always loaded down with more food than they could possibly eat at one sitting. I couldn't get over that. Most of the time they had food left over. At our house there were never any leftovers and we often went away still hungry. Of course I knew the reason for the difference. Audrey's father had a job. In a bank.

They usually ate early because Mr. Westover finished work at four o'clock. He'd drive all the way from downtown Toronto to east-end Birchcliff in his 1929 Model A Ford. It was the only car on Lilac Street, and when it came rattling round the corner blaring *AhhOOgaa!* kids would run like stink from all directions and jump on the running board for a free ride.

Sometimes Mrs. Westover let me sit on the back kitchen steps and pat the dog while Audrey ate her supper. Spot was a friendly Boston Bull. Mrs. Westover said he had a pedigree, but I looked him over from his pushed-in nose to his twisty tail and I couldn't find a thing wrong with him. Spot ate the very same food as the rest of the family. Just smelling his lovely, meaty dish was enough to make me drool.

Often, after supper, Mrs. Westover would offer me the leftovers. "So it won't go to waste," she'd say offhandedly. But I knew it was her way of being charitable without making me feel my neck. She was nice, Mrs. Westover. Audrey's father was nice too. He never seemed to mind how much food his wife gave away. Not even once did I see that "What's going on here?" look cross his face. Sometimes he even joked with me. I think he liked me.

On this particular night I came galloping back down the street with my hoop and stick under my arm, half a store-bought apple pie in one hand and a loaf of yesterday's bread in the other. Mum was pleased as punch.

Dad came in the back door right behind me. He always came home about the same time as the working men. He looked tired and thin. Under his wispy fair hair his square-jawed face was pale and drawn.

"Hi, Dad!" I gave him a toothy grin to cheer him up.

"Hello, Bea," he answered without a trace of a smile.

Everybody was home now, so we all sat down around the oilcloth-covered table. All except little Jakey who still used a high chair.

There was no butter on the table, so we dipped our bread in the stew Mum had made. Boy, she made good stew! Even without meat. We sopped up every drop until the last crust of bread was gone and our plates were shiny clean. Then Mum divided the pie into six skinny pieces. Dad said he was full and didn't want any. Even I didn't believe that. He just wanted us kids to have his share. So Arthur and I obliged by fighting over it. Willa left the table in disgust. Mum settled the argument by giving the extra piece to me. Arthur got mad and stomped out of the room.

"The school nurse says Bea is a bit underweight," explained Mum, trying to sound casual. "She can do with something extra."

"I've *got* to get a job!" declared Dad for the umpteenth time.

I finished the sliver of pie in no time flat. Then, seeing Mum and Dad looking depressed over their tea, I said, "Don't worry, Mum. You neither, Dad. I'm strong as a horse—watch!"

Willa was at the sink with her back to me, doing the dishes. I crept up behind her and lifted her bodily off the floor. She must have outweighed me by fifty pounds at least. It felt more like a ton. But I had to prove how strong I was so I hung on, staggering backwards.

"Bea! You put me down!" screeched Willa.

I could hardly wait to oblige. I thought I was going to faint, and I must have turned white because Mum looked scared and made me sit right down and have a sip of tea.

"Tea revives you," she said.

"Don't you do that again!" Dad said with a show of anger. "You might have broken your back, you foolish girl."

But I think it made them feel a bit more cheerful, just the same, because they didn't have their usual fight after supper.

# 2

# My big confession

Willa finished up the dishes and wiped around the sink and stove. Then she folded the dish towel neatly and hung it on the drying rack. Getting her books from her school bag, she settled herself at the dining room table to do her homework. Arthur followed her example. They were both good students, but Willa was the extra-clever one.

Two years before, in Senior Fourth, she had won the gold medal for achieving highest honours in Scarborough's high school entrance examinations. Hundreds of kids had competed—and our Willa had won.

Mum and Dad were proud as punch and couldn't stop bragging about her. On and on they went until all our friends and relations were sick and tired of listening. Poor Willa. She was absolutely mortified. Finally, she hid the gold medal in a secret place, and when Mum asked her where it was so she could show it one more time, Willa wouldn't tell. She could be stubborn when she felt like it.

I was proud of Willa too, but it was awfully hard on me, having such a clever sister. Her picture, with the medal pinned to her blouse, hung in the hallway of Birchcliff Public School and my teacher would never let me forget it. Every time I got a bad mark in arithmetic, which was nearly every day, Miss Birchall would raise her shaggy eyebrows and exclaim for everyone to hear, "Surely *you* can't be Willa Thomson's sister?"

She knew darn well I was. Her sarcasm shrivelled my soul.

It was hard on Arthur, too, having a gold medallist for a sister, but in a different way. Arthur was smart enough and he always got good marks, but his teacher and the principal were never satisfied. They kept at him to work harder and do better so he, too, would win a medal and bring honour to the school. At least I was spared that kind of torture. If I had liked him better I would have felt downright sorry for him.

Everybody knew from my daily zeros in arithmetic that I was a hopeless scholar. Miss Birchall even said that if I didn't soon improve I might lose the whole year. That threat scared the daylights out of me so I begged Willa to help me.

She tried, she really did. But the minute I saw all those numbers on the page my brain went numb. In desperation I'd count on my fingers under the table. Then Willa would catch me and bawl me out and I'd start to cry and leave the table in disgrace.

Once I got up the nerve to ask Miss Birchall, "Why can't I just pass in spelling and reading and composition? Why is arithmetic so important?"

"Because it takes *brains* to do arithmetic!" she snorted, withering me with that look. "Any ninny can get good marks in spelling and composition."

After that I knew I was sunk. I couldn't make head nor tail out of arithmetic, especially problems. Who but a wallpaper man needed to know how many rolls it took to paper a room nine by twelve anyway?

That night I sat with Arthur and Willa and tried to learn my nine times-table. They took no notice of me, except from time to time Arthur gave me a dirty look for sniffling my nose. So I'd stare him down and he'd stick out his tongue; then we'd both go back to our books.

Just looking at Arthur made me sick. He was such a handsome, well-behaved twelve-year-old. The kind grown-ups, especially ladies, really take to.

Actually we looked a lot alike, since we both favoured Dad's side, but Arthur was prettier than I was. He had blond curly hair (mine was blonde too, but dead straight), big blue eyes (mine were the same colour, but not so big), a neat nose and white even teeth (my nose was too big and my front teeth were saw-edged—Mum said they would wear smooth in time but it hadn't happened yet).

Willa was nice looking too. She had Mum's dark wavy hair and Dad's blue eyes and fair skin. Everybody said it was a lovely combination and she'd start to "turn heads" any day now.

There was only one thing I liked about myself. It was my flat chest. Poor Willa had breasts and she had to wear a tight undershirt to hide them. Every night I thanked God for my flat chest and begged Him not to give me breasts.

Pretty soon I got tired of the nine times-table and Arthur's dirty looks, so I asked Mum if I could get Jakey ready for bed. She let out a big sigh and said yes. Then Dad went down the cellar and put a boilerful of water on the gas plate.

Jakey was the baby of our family. He was the only one who favoured Mum's side. He had big brown eyes, dark curly hair and dimples, just like her. And there was a special tie between

Mum and Jakey—I mean over and above the fact that he looked like her.

When he was a tiny baby he took sick and nearly died. The sickness was called "summer complaint" and when little babies get it they have diarrhea and their milk won't stay down. Then they lose all their body water and they die. Most of them. But our baby was lucky. Mum and Dad rushed him down to Sick Children's Hospital as fast as the streetcars would go and Mum gave him a blood transfusion that saved his life.

Dad was mad because they wouldn't use his blood. The doctors said it was the wrong type. "How can that be when I'm the father?" Dad demanded angrily. So the doctors explained, as best they could, that children don't always inherit their father's blood. They said a transfusion from Dad might even kill Jakey (who was nearly dead already) so Dad had to give in, but he never really got over it.

Mum told us all about it when they got home. "I laid on a stretcher and they put Jakey on a table right beside me. Then they put a needle in my arm and a needle in Jakey's little ankle and a glass tube joined us together. I could see my blood flowing into his tiny, white foot. He was so weak he didn't even cry. Poor little gaffer—they 'bused him."

"What does 'boozed' mean, Mum?" I asked, all agog.

"It means abused, hurt. My mother used to say that when she heard a baby cry."

Poor Mum. She always blamed herself for Jakey's illness because the doctors at Sick Kids' said it was caused from unboiled milk. Of course Mum didn't know that milk needed to be boiled to be purified, but she said ignorance was no excuse. So she went to the library and got all the newest medical books and wrote down as many of the latest remedies as she could find.

All that attention made me terribly jealous of Jakey. In fact, I had been jealous of him right from the start. And no wonder. The very day he was born, upstairs in the middle bedroom, Dad dropped me like a hot potato. It was the shock of my life. For six years I had been the youngest and had been treated kind of special. Particularly by Dad. He used to dandle me on his knee and piggyback me around the yard and dance with me standing on his shoes. Then along came Jakey.

He was a beautiful baby. And he was a boy! That's when it first dawned on me how all-fired special it was to be a boy. Dad kept saying, "It's a boy! A boy! I've got another son!" You'd have thought it was a god from heaven instead of just an ordinary, everyday baby.

Everybody congratulated Dad and told him how lucky he was. And Uncle Charlie, Dad's brother, who was going to be a father soon himself, said that if his baby was a girl he'd send it back where it came from.

He laughed when he said it, as if it was a joke, but Willa and I were standing right there and we didn't think it was funny.

We looked each other up and down to see what was wrong with us. I already knew I wasn't the kind of child grown-ups were dying to have, but why on earth wouldn't anybody want Willa? She was just about perfect as children go.

I was awfully disappointed in Uncle Charlie. He had been my favourite uncle up till then. I never dreamed he didn't like Willa and me because we were girls. And what a dumb reason! God made us, didn't He? He must have known what He was doing. And as for my dad, well, I just couldn't get over it. So I took all my hurt feelings out on poor little Jakey.

I'd pinch him when no one was looking, just to hear him cry. I'd bump his cot when he was sound asleep. And I'd grab the bottle out of his mouth in the middle of a suck. Then, when he got older, I discovered that sad songs made him cry. So I'd sing to him by the hour. Songs like "The Letter Edged In Black" and "Hello Central, Give Me Heaven" and "Climb Upon My Knee Sonny Boy."

Mum thought I was being a nice big sister, singing to my baby brother, but I wasn't. I was being awful. Finally my guilty conscience got the better of me. I couldn't sleep for thinking about how terrible I was. So I decided to snitch on myself.

The opportunity came one day when Miss Birchall had a gumboil and had to go to the dentist. For once I got out of school early, so I ran all the way home to catch my mum alone.

It was Tuesday, so she was ironing. She was just folding up Arthur's Sunday shirt as I came in the door. It was stiff with starch and gleaming white. Except for the frayed collar, it looked brand-new out of the store.

Scuffling nervously, I made my confession.

"I'm glad you told me, Bea," she said thoughtfully, tipping the iron on end. "It shows you're not mean at heart. You just leave it with me. I'll speak to your father. And I'll give that Charlie a piece of my mind, you can bet your boots on that."

She tested the iron with a wet finger. It hissed and she cried "Ouch!" and pulled the plug out of the wall. Sucking the burnt finger, she smoothed a threadbare flannelette sheet over the board and continued, "Now, don't be mean to Jakey any more,

Bea. It's not his fault, you know. He can't help being a boy any more than you can help being a girl."

"Oh, don't worry, Mum, I won't." I felt good all over now that the weight was off my chest. "I'll make it up to him, you'll see. But Mum, are boys better than girls?"

Sparks flew from her big brown eyes and the iron moved in quick, angry strokes. "No, they're not. And don't you think it. Some of them aren't half as good. Why, I wouldn't trade you or Willa for all the boys in China!"

"Are we even better than Arthur and Jakey?" If she said yes, I could hardly wait to tell Arthur.

"Not on your tintype!" she said emphatically. "Nobody is better than my boys. But you're every bit as good, and don't you forget it." Setting the iron on end, she gave me an unexpected bone-cracker.

"And another thing you should bear in mind, Bea: this old world is changing, especially since the war. When I was a girl women didn't even have the vote, and only boys were encouraged to get an education. See how different things are now? Just look at your own sister—a gold medallist, halfway through high school and her not even fifteen years old. Girls can be anything they want to be nowadays, Bea. Why, only last spring—May, I think it was—a girl named Amelia Earhart flew across the Atlantic Ocean all by herself. Now doesn't that beat all? And another thing, Booky, these hard times aren't going to last forever, you know. There'll be jobs galore just begging for qualified people some day. Mark my words. So you just work hard and get an education and grow up to be somebody!"

The part about working hard and getting an education worried me a bit. But the part about the lady flyer made my imagination soar. I decided then and there to be an aeroplane pilot when I grew up.

That little talk cured me forever of my jealousy. From that minute on I was nice to Jakey, and soon he loved me best of all.

But one thing I forgot to ask, something I was dying to know and I missed my chance again. If Uncle Charlie's baby was a girl, where would he send her back to?

# 3

# An awful fight

It was that same night, very late, when I woke from a cosy sleep to the sound of my parents' angry voices. Cold shivers crept over me. I couldn't get used to their fighting, even though it happened nearly every day.

I buried my head under the pillow, trying not to hear. But it was stuffy under there and I had to come up for air. They were shouting now—terrible, ugly, fighting words. The kind that lead to blows. I didn't know what to do.

I looked at Willa. She was dead to the world on her back. Her mouth was open and she was snoring. She had a loud snore.

I got up and tiptoed down the hall. Feeling around for the string, I pulled the hall light on. The pale glow lit the staircase and spilled into the boys' room. Arthur was sound asleep, one foot hanging over the edge of the thin, felt mattress. Jakey was curled up beside him, his rump sticking up, his thumb loosely in his mouth. He looked so sweet and clean, the damp, dark ringlets clinging to his little round head. No one would ever dream he'd wet up Arthur's back every single night.

Suddenly a piercing shriek came ringing up the stairs. Then a loud thump, like a fist hitting the table.

I streaked down the stairs and stopped short at the bottom, grabbing the banister post for support. Under my thin cotton nightdress I shook like an autumn leaf. My heart skipped in my chest and gooseflesh crept all over my body.

The front rooms were in darkness. I could just make out the school books piled neatly on the round table. Only the kitchen light was on, a single forty-watt bulb dangling on a black wire from the high ceiling.

My parents hadn't seen me yet. Mum sat at the table, head thrown back, glaring defiantly up into Dad's ashen face. Her cheeks were beet red. His were sidewalk grey.

*"No!"* he roared at her. "I won't agree to give it up, no matter what you say."

"All you're thinking about is yourself," Mum retorted bitterly. "You're just concerned about what people will say. Well, I don't care what anybody says just so long as it has a good home, proper food, a chance for an education. We're lucky such a fine family wants it."

"What kind of a woman are you anyway?" Dad hissed, spraying Mum's face with spit. "No *real* woman would give up her own flesh and blood."

I saw Mum wince at the cruel words.

"It's not what I want, you fool!" Her voice shook with rage. "We can barely feed the four we've got. This one is unborn— unnamed. If we give it up right away . . ." Her hand touched her stomach, gently, protectively, the way she sometimes touched my face. It was only then that I noticed how huge her stomach was.

Her head jerked up and she looked Dad straight in the eye. "Isn't it bad enough that the ones we've got are underweight and undernourished?" she said coldly.

"I'll get work! I'll get money! I'll get them what they need!"

"Talk's cheap!"

"Shut up, if you know what's good for you!" Dad's fist jabbed the air just inches from Mum's nose.

My feet took wings. Flying through the darkened rooms, I landed with a thud at Mum's side. If it came to a showdown, which it often did, I was my mother's girl.

Shaking from head to foot, I began to shriek between them. "Mum! Dad! Is it a baby? Are we going to get a baby?" I didn't wait for an answer. "Please, Mum, don't give it away. I won't eat so much any more. It can have half my food. I like being underweight. Honest! You can run way faster when you're skinny."

They stared dumbfounded for a minute; then Mum reached out and put an arm around me. Dad's fist seemed to come down in slow motion. Moaning softly, he slumped to a chair and buried his head on the table.

"Don't cry, Dad." I touched his bony shoulder gingerly. "Willa and Arthur and me, we'll help, you'll see."

I had no idea what I meant by help. All I knew was that I had to prevent the awful fight from starting up again.

The colour had drained from Mum's cheeks, leaving them a pale yellow. One arm was still around me. The other was draped over her swollen middle.

I dared to poke it with my index finger. To my surprise, it was as hard as a baseball.

"Is it really in there, Mum?"

She nodded with a wry smile.

"Don't give it away!"

"Don't you worry your head, Booky."

But she didn't promise. Rising awkwardly, she went to put the latch on the door. Dad stood on the chair and unscrewed the light bulb to take upstairs. The one in their bedroom had burned out weeks ago.

Silently we climbed the stairs, Mum pulling herself, breathlessly, hand over hand on the banister.

I crept into bed beside Willa. She was still on her back but she wasn't snoring. Her eyes were wide open, glistening in the darkness.

"Do you know where babies come from, Willa?" I whispered.

"Yes."

I could barely hear her.

"So do I," I said importantly. But there was one more thing I needed to know. "How will it get out?"

"Go to sleep," ordered Willa.

So I did.

# 4

# Thank goodness for Hallowe'en

By the time Hallowe'en came, I was really down in the dumps. Mum and Dad fought nearly every day and every time Dad went slamming out the door he left behind him a cloud of gloom. It was nearly as bad as when there's a death in the family and the body is laid out in the parlour, which is what the front room is called when someone is laid out in it.

Ordinarily my spirits would bounce right back no matter what, but this time they had hit rock bottom. So thank goodness for Hallowe'en.

Mum warned me not to get too excited about it this year. She said 1932 would be a bad year for shelling out. Our front room blinds were already pulled down, so the neighbourhood kids would know we couldn't afford to shell out this year. The darkened windows would keep the kids away just as surely as if a red *Scarlet Fever* sign were tacked to the front door.

But still I could hardly wait to dress up, as I always did on All Hallow's Eve, in my brother's old clothes. It was my favourite costume, my special daydream, my once-a-year chance to be a boy.

When Mum saw me getting ready she said, "Bea, wouldn't

you like to be a ghost for a change? There's an old sheet down in the laundry basket you could use."

"Oh, no, Mum!" I protested. "Don't you see? If I be a ghost this year I'll have to wait another whole year to be a boy!"

"I see," she said, giving my nose a little pinch that made it stick together.

When I was all ready I surveyed myself in Mum's bureau mirror. In his jacket and breeches, with my short, fair hair tucked up under his peaked cap, I was the dead-spit of Arthur. I even felt like him. I guess I wished I *was* him, but I would have yanked my tongue out by the roots rather than admit it.

Pulling on my black linen eye mask and grabbing my Eaton's shopping bag, I ran up the street to Audrey's. A few lighted pumpkins glimmered in the windows of Lilac Street. They stood out like friendly beacons in the dark, chilly night.

Audrey's jack-o'-lantern grinned invitingly from their front porch window. Her mother gave us our first shellout: a rosy McIntosh apple and three candy kisses. "Now, don't you girls go anywhere near the Morris house," she warned at the door. "That mean Mr. Morris threw out red-hot pennies last year and some of the neighbourhood boys were badly burned."

I knew this was true because Arthur was one of the boys. Mum had been mad as hops about it and had even gone down to the police station. But nothing came of it. "That's because old Morris is a monied man," Dad complained bitterly. "The rich, they think they're above the law."

Now the streets were milling with strange, exciting creatures: ghosts and goblins, witches and scarecrows, all drawn to the lighted houses like moths to a flame.

"Do you like my costume, Bea?" asked Audrey, twirling

around so her bride's veil and long sausage curls floated out behind her on the autumn breeze.

"It's gorgeous!" I replied obligingly. "Do you like mine?" I touched the peak of my cap like a gentleman.

"Oh, Bea!" Audrey screwed her nose up scornfully. "It's not a costume. It's only your brother's old suit."

"All right for you, Audrey!" I cried threateningly. But I let it go at that. I didn't want anything to spoil Hallowe'en.

Our first stop was Mrs. Cook's house. Mrs. Cook was known far and wide as the best shell-outer in Birchcliff. But there was a catch to it: you had to pass a test. Everyone was marched into her brightly lit kitchen and ordered to unmask. This yearly ritual scared the daylights out of me because I always had such a darned old guilty conscience!

"Ah, it's you, Beatrice," said Mrs. Cook, towering over me, her flabby arms folded over her big bosom. "For a minute there I thought you were Arthur. Well now, I don't recall you doing any mischief around my property this past summer, so you may put your mask back on and help yourself."

Miraculously, I had passed again. I knew perfectly well I had taken shortcuts across her green-carpet lawn and flying leaps over her flowerbeds during the summer, but I vowed then and there never to do it again.

Audrey passed too, so we both went to the treat-laden table. We ate a mouth-watering piece of chocolate cake on the spot. Then into our bags went a Dad's oatmeal cookie (I took two and Audrey looked disgusted—sometimes she reminded me of Willa), a big piece of vanilla fudge wrapped in waxed paper, a caramel popcorn ball and a taffy apple.

On our way out we remembered to say thank you. Mrs. Cook

looked up from the new bunch she was testing. "Oh, you're welcome, dears. See you next year."

"Shell out! Shell out! The witches are out!" cried a tramp and a clown on the doorstep. "Did you pass?" they whispered anxiously.

"Sure, it was easy!" we boasted.

I don't think any kid was ever turned away from Mrs. Cook's table, but all of us quaked at the possibility.

Off we went, Audrey and me, to scour the neighbourhood for lighted houses. Little by little our bags grew heavy. Mum had been wrong about 1932.

On Warden Avenue we stopped to catch our breath and eat a minty humbug. It had begun to rain, a fine Hallowe'en drizzle. Across the street we saw a bunch of boys who looked as if they were up to mischief. One of them crept over to our side and up onto a dark verandah.

"That's old man Morris's house," whispered Audrey.

Cold shivers ran up my spine. Noiselessly the boy fastened something to the door; then he quickly backtracked, playing out a ball of twine. When I saw his face under the streetlight I recognized, of all people, my own brother Arthur.

"Arthur! Arthur! What are you doing?" I screeched.

"Shut your trap, Bea!"

One of the other boys came over and shook his fist in my face. "Beat it if you don't want a bloody nose," he growled.

"You leave her alone, Tommy," hissed Arthur. "She's my sister." I could hardly believe my ears!

The boys hid in a clump of spirea and began to jerk the string. *Tap, tap, tap,* went the door knocker. No answer. "Pull harder!*" Bang! Bang! Bang!* Suddenly the door flew open and out leapt old man Morris, yelling his head off.

Audrey and I turned tail and ran. The last thing I saw, over my shoulder, was the old man tumbling head-over-heels down his verandah steps and the gang of boys scattering in all directions.

We didn't stop running until we got in sight of Audrey's house. By this time her bride's costume was a bedraggled mess, but the rain hadn't hurt Arthur's old suit one bit.

Her mother was peering anxiously out the window. The candle in their pumpkin had gone out. The minute she saw us she came to the door and said, "For mercy's sake, Audrey, don't you know enough to come in out of the rain?" Then to me, "You get right home, Beatrice." So I did.

Mum was sitting in the middle of the kitchen under the light bulb mending a ladder in her stocking. They were her only pair of real silk so she had to make them last. With threads picked from an old pair, and using a fine needle, she'd weave her way up the long ladder. When she was finished the run would have disappeared like magic.

Willa was making corrugated insoles on the table. She pressed her shoe on the cardboard and traced the outline with a pencil. Then she cut it out and fitted it over the hole inside her shoe.

I dumped my whole bag of treats beside her insoles on the table and told them both to help themselves. Mum chose the piece of fudge. Willa picked a licorice stick. Then Mum said I should keep the rest for myself, but I gave her all my apples, except the taffy apple.

"Glory be," she declared. "I'll make a lovely Brown-Betty tomorrow."

Bone weary but happy, I dragged my soggy bag up the stairs and hid it under the bed for safekeeping. Then I climbed out of Arthur's damp suit and into my nice dry nightdress. It felt good to be a girl again.

After a while I heard Willa come up. She splashed in the bathroom for ages. She was always washing herself, even when she wasn't dirty.

"Did you like your licorice stick?" I asked when she finally slipped into bed beside me.

"You smell, Bea!" she said, ignoring my bid for praise. "Why can't you wash your feet at least?"

Boy, did that make me mad! But I couldn't help feeling sorry for her. It must be awful to be too big to go out on Hallowe'en.

The next day the school was buzzing with rumours about a bunch of boys who had done a pile of mischief around the neighbourhood. Baby buggies were found dangling from telephone poles, backhouses were knocked over (old Mr. Peebles was sitting in his at the time!), and bad words were scribbled with soap all over the store windows on Kingston Road. But worst of all, old man Morris had broken his collarbone when he fell down his verandah steps while chasing some mischief-makers.

By the time we got home from school Mum knew all about it. Then, at the supper table, she told the whole story to Dad. Of course she never dreamed that her darling Arthur had anything to do with it.

While she talked Arthur kept darting pleading looks across the table. Boy, was I tempted. It was the chance of a lifetime to get back at him for all the mean things he had done to me in the past. For sure he'd get the razor-strop if Dad found out.

Dad was very strict about some things, like respecting other people's property and not saucing back your elders and things like that. He had some funny notions about discipline too. For instance, if we got the strap in school, he'd strap us when we got home, for getting the strap in school. Mum said that was a barbaric practice and she wouldn't have any part of it. So if we got the strap (better known as the slugs) Mum would hush it up and Dad would never find out. Of course Willa never got the slugs, and Arthur very seldom, but I got them regularly for my zeros in arithmetic.

When Dad first heard about Mr. Morris's broken collarbone his lips twitched and he said, "Serves him right, the old demon." Then he thought better of it and added, "Still, I don't hold with wilful mischief. Do you know anything about this, Arthur?"

Arthur started to choke on a crust of bread and Mum jumped up and thumped him on the back. "No, Dad!" he lied, his face going blotchy red.

Dad turned to me. "Beatrice?"

Temptation reared its ugly head again. Then I remembered my last razor-stropping. I had followed a parade down to the city limits and I hadn't got home until after dark. Willa sent me straight to bed and told me to pretend I was asleep. I did, but it didn't do any good. Dad roared up the stairs, yanked down the covers, threw up my nightdress and stropped my bare behind. I couldn't sit down for a week.

I decided I didn't want revenge that bad. And besides, hadn't Arthur saved me from a punch in the nose and admitted right out loud in front of all his friends that I was his sister? "No, Dad, I didn't see anything. Audrey and I were too busy shelly-outing. See the swell Brown-Betty Mum made from my apples?"

"It looks good, Bea," he said, smacking his lips.

After the Hallowe'en night, when Arthur stuck up for me and I didn't tell on him, we liked each other better. Not much, but some.

# 5

# Commotion
# in the night

I was a terrible trial to Willa, I really was. The only thing we had in common was the old iron bed we shared. We didn't talk to each other much. There wasn't anything to say. She was five years older than I was, but that wasn't the worst of it. She was neat and clean and smart and sensible. I was messy and scatterbrained—and dumb in arithmetic.

The thing I did that bothered her most was going to bed with dirty stockings on. The smell nearly drove her crazy. And my running shoes were twice as bad as my stockings. I could hardly stand them myself. Almost every night, in the summertime, Willa would pitch them out the window. Then in the morning I'd have to go out in the brambles, barefoot, to find them.

Of course, I wasn't *allowed* to go to bed dirty. Far from it. I guess my mother was the cleanest woman in the world, but when she sent me up to take a bath, and after Dad had lugged a boilerful of scalding water up two flights of stairs, I'd just sit on the toilet seat daydreaming and yanking on the chain of the water closet overhead, listening to "Niagara Falls."

Then, when the water in the tub had turned stone cold, I'd

pull the plug, give my face and hands a "lick and a promise," put on my clean nightdress and hop happily into bed. Poor Willa. How she wished I had been born a boy so I would have to sleep with Arthur.

The night the new baby was born it was November and too cold to throw my running shoes out the window, so she scolded me unmercifully instead.

I cried myself to sleep and woke up to a strange commotion going on in the hallway. There was a muffled cry that trailed off in a long shuddering moan. It sounded like my mother's voice. Then, straining my ears, I heard an unfamiliar male voice saying terrible things. "Strap her down! Hold on to her legs! Give her another whiff. Cover her nose and mouth."

The awful words made no sense to me at all, but they struck cold terror into my heart. Leaping out of bed, I streaked down the hall screaming at the top of my lungs, "Mum! Mum! Mum!"

Dad caught me by my nightdress and smacked my skinny behind.

"Get back to bed and shut the door!" His voice was a rasping whisper.

Shaking like a bowlful of jelly, I dove back in beside Willa, and crept as close to her as I dared.

"What's the matter, Willa?" I whispered fearfully. "What's happening to Mum?"

"It's the baby," she said quietly.

"The baby? In Mum's stomach? Is it trying to get out? Is it hurting Mum? Why are they strapping her?"

"Shut up!" she snapped, and I couldn't get another word out of her. She just lay there, perfectly still, staring up at the ceiling.

I gave up and buried my head under the pillow, plugging my ears with my fingers. It was pitch dark under there, but I saw lights, orange and blue and red, sailing in all directions like fireworks on the 24th of May.

I must have gone to sleep finally, because the next thing I knew it was morning and I was all alone in the bed. The house was as quiet as a church on Monday. Dressing in a flash, my heart in my mouth, I crept down the hall past the closed door of my parents' room.

The kitchen light was on. I could tell the stove was lit by the lovely warmth wafting through the dining room. I heard spoons clinking and whispered conversation. Then I saw Aunt Myrtle, Uncle Charlie's wife, her bulging apron pressed against the stove, stirring something in the grey graniteware saucepan. (She was in the family way, too. I knew all about that at last!)

"Good morning, Bea," she greeted me pleasantly. "How would you like another baby brother?"

For a second there I thought I had a choice. "I'd rather have a sister this time," I answered innocently.

"Well, like it or not, you've got another brother."

"Dumb-bell!" hissed Arthur.

Aunt Myrtle filled my bowl with thick, grey porridge. "You can go up to see him before you go to school," she said.

She was nice, Aunt Myrtle; we all liked her. But she sure was a terrible cook. Her porridge was as lumpy and tasteless as wallpaper paste (which I had sampled once when Dad papered our bedroom). Mum's porridge was always creamy white with brown sugar sprinkled on it.

"What's wrong with the porridge, Willa?" I whispered.

"She forgot the salt. Be quiet and eat."

Arthur sat, hunched over, spooning in the lumps. Instead of porridge, Jakey was greedily devouring a bowl of bready milk. He'd rather have bready milk than porridge any day. And if there wasn't any milk he'd cheerfully settle for bready water, just as long as there was brown sugar sprinkled on it.

I noticed a dish of butter in the middle of the table. Aunt Myrtle must have brought it for a treat. So I made myself a white sugar sandwich. Mmm, it was good, the way the sugar mixed with the salty yellow butter. Satisfied at last, I jumped up and headed for the stairs.

I could hardly wait to see the baby and my mother. I needed to see for myself if she was all right. Easing open the bedroom door, I peeked in. Mum's eyes were like dark coals in white snow. Her hair was like a black cloud on the pillow. She gave me a weak smile and held out her hand.

I crept on tiptoe to the laundry basket perched on a chair beside her bed. The baby was asleep, wrapped in a napkin and lying on a pillow. He was the worst looking baby I'd ever laid eyes on. He was as skinny as a plucked chicken and he had a lump on the side of his head the size of a teacup. I didn't know what to say, so I blurted out, "Has he got a name, Mum?"

"No, Bea. Can you think of one?" Her voice was low and gravelly.

I thought for a minute. I liked double names myself. Hyphenated. Like Anna-Belle or Betty-Ann. My doll's name was Margaret-Mae (after Grampa Thomson's two milk cows). Once I had asked Mum if she would mind calling me both my names, Beatrice-Myrtle (after Aunt Myrtle). I hated them both, but I thought the hyphen improved them quite a bit. "Oh, Bea, that's too much of a mouthful!" Mum had said, even though I'd explained that the hyphen made it all one word.

"Could we give him a double name, Mum?" I decided to try again. "How about William Robert? And we could call him Billy-Bob for short."

"William is a nice name, after Puppa. I like Robert too. I think Billy will suit him just fine."

I guess she didn't like double names.

Just then Dad came into the room. He was wearing the same pleased expression as the day Jakey was born. But this time it didn't bother me. He rested his hand on my head and we looked in the basket together. I told him the names I had picked and he said he liked them.

Just then the baby opened his big blue eyes and stared straight up at me. I think he knew me! My heart swelled with love and pride. Then I remembered the awful night when Mum and Dad were fighting about giving him away.

"Mum, Dad, you won't give him away, will you?" Before Dad had a chance to open his mouth, Mum said, "Don't you worry your head about that anymore, Booky. The minute I saw him I knew I could never part with him."

I knew I could believe her. I leaned over the bed and she held me tight. Her lips were hot and dry on my forehead. Dad kissed me too, and I tasted butter on his mouth.

Reaching inside the basket with my little finger, I touched the baby's velvet cheek. Then I ran off to school.

# 6

# A special
# birthday present

I could hardly wait to tell Audrey. Boy, would she be surprised!

Hurrying up the street, my head ducked against the cold east wind, I thought of something funny. It was my birthday and nobody had remembered. Not much wonder with all the goings-on at our house that night. Then I thought of something else. Mum had said Billy arrived right after midnight. That meant he had been born on my birthday. He was my birthday present—a real live baby doll. I felt a tug at my heart at the thought of him, my funny looking, skinny little, bumpy-headed, brand new brother. Then and there I knew he would always be special to me.

The weather had turned raw and ice was on the puddles. But it hadn't snowed yet, if you didn't count a little flurry.

Mrs. Westover let me wait in the back kitchen out of the cold. I didn't say a word while Audrey got her snowsuit on. It was a matching snowsuit, three pieces, the first I'd ever seen. Audrey always had the latest fashions. I was wearing my blue coat that Mum had made over for me from cousin Lottie's. My legs were all covered in duck-bumps where my brown ribbed stockings and navy blue bloomers didn't quite meet.

"Hey, Mrs. Westover," I couldn't hold it in any longer, "guess how many kids there are in my family."

She knitted her brows thoughtfully. "Why, there are four, aren't there? Two boys and two girls."

"No," I squealed gleefully, "there's five! Last night my mother borned a new baby boy. His name is Billy, short for William, after Grampa Cole. I named him and he's mine because he was born on my birthday."

"Oh, your poor dear mother," cried Mrs. Westover, her fat pudgy hand with the big diamond ring fluttering to her bosom.

At first I thought she meant Mum was poor because she didn't have a diamond ring (Mum didn't even have a wedding band right now because she had pawned it to buy coal). But then I realized she was feeling sorry for Mum because she had a new baby. I was never so taken aback. I expected her to be all in a twitter and offer me congratulations. After all, how many kids get a new baby brother for their birthday?

But instead she acted as if I had brought her bad news. I couldn't understand it. And then it struck me. She was jealous—and no wonder. She had only Audrey, and Mum had all of us. Just the same I was disappointed in Mrs. Westover. So I decided if we ever got another new baby she wouldn't be the first to know.

Audrey wasn't a whole lot better. I thought she'd be all ears to hear about the strange goings-on at our house in the middle of the night. I started to tell her all about it as we crossed the windy field leading out onto Kingston Road, but she didn't seem the least bit interested. She just kept changing the subject to the lamb's wool coat her father was having made for her mother for Christmas. She was all excited about it because he said there would be enough fur left over to trim a coat for her. And maybe a muff too!

That sure knocked the wind out of my sails. But not for long. After all, my new coat had a fur collar too. Rabbit. When Cousin Lottie heard I didn't have a winter coat she came right over with her old one and said it was just the excuse she was looking for to buy herself a new one.

Lottie was a spinster and she had a steady job at Simpson's. Everybody made fun of her for not being married, and teased her about not being able to catch a man (which surprised me because Lottie was a good runner. I had seen her win lots of races at our Sunday School picnics). But she didn't care. She said no man was going to sweet-talk her into being a slave to a bunch of kids and a washboard. Mum said Cousin Lottie had a good head on her shoulders.

The coat was huge, like Lottie herself, and Mum had a hard job cutting it up and making it down to fit skinny little me. And all the while she worked, her right foot flying on the treadle, she kept saying over and over that she hoped she had enough time to get done. I didn't know what she meant at the time, but now I understood that the baby was due soon.

© Eaton's Archives

And to make matters

worse, the trial period for the sewing machine had already run out. Not only was Mum expecting a baby any minute, but she was also expecting the horse-drawn Eaton's wagon to pull up to the door and repossess the precious sewing machine.

But she finished my coat in the nick of time, and it was beautiful. Lottie said it was a work of art, and she went right out and bought me a blue toque and mittens to match. I was proud as punch of myself, all decked out in my favourite colour. If it hadn't been for my stockings and bloomers not quite meeting, I would have been as warm as toast.

So Audrey and her mother didn't dampen my spirits for long. After all, I had a new winter outfit and a new baby brother. And I was ten years old and Audrey was still only nine.

* * *

Billy fast caught up to Jakey in the cute department, but without a word of a lie he was the crabbiest kid in creation. If there had been a contest for the world's most crotchety baby, I'll bet our Billy would have won first prize, easy.

Mum made up all kinds of excuses for his crankiness. "They 'bused him," she'd say, or, "He's got a touch of gripes," or, "He's hungry, poor little gaffer. He never seems to get enough to eat."

Well, he wasn't the only one. We were all famished most of the time. Dad said the "pogey" would hardly keep body and soul together. I guess that's why those years were called the hungry thirties.

By this time I was convinced that our baby wouldn't be given away ("He cries so much, who'd want him?" as Willa pointed out), but the fear of losing him still dogged me in my dreams. Morning after morning I'd wake to find myself squeezed into

his little iron cot with my arms wrapped protectively around him. I never knew how I got there and it soon became a family joke.

Dad would say, "Bea went for a jaunt last night and guess where she ended up?" Then they'd all laugh and tease me. But I didn't mind. It was all in fun.

My spare time was so taken up with Billy, helping Mum bath him and taking him for rides and jiggling his cot to make him sleep, that I almost forgot Christmas was just around the corner. I had never been that carried away with anything in my life before.

# 7

# "Hello, Bluebird"

If I live to be a hundred, I'll always bless Eaton's for the Santa Claus Parade. In my opinion, Santa Claus Parade Day was second only to Christmas Day and third to Hallowe'en. And best of all, it was absolutely free.

But Dad said in a pig's eye it was free. He said it was nothing but a big conspiracy by the rich capitalist Eaton Company against the downtrodden poor of Toronto. He always managed to put a damper on the great event by ranting and raving like that.

"What's a conspiracy, Dad?" Arthur was interested in things like that. "And what's a capitalist?"

"Conspiracy is when Eaton's makes poor children hanker after things their parents can't afford," was Dad's gloomy explanation. "And capitalism means that the rich get richer and the poor get poorer."

But he hadn't forgotten altogether what it meant to be a child at Christmas time. He never failed to take us to the parade.

We were up before daylight on that wonderful day, excitedly eating our porridge by the dim glow of the light bulb.

"Eat up," Mum urged us, "so you'll be well fortified against the cold."

And cold it was. Bitter winds swept across Kingston Road from the golf links, chilling us to the bone. The "radio" car went rattling by, its lucky passengers peering out through round peepholes made by warm fingers on frosty windows. But it cost an extra nickel to ride, so we couldn't afford it.

Miraculously, a streetcar was waiting at the city limits. We clambered up the wooden steps and hurried past the driver to the middle of the car where a little square stove nestled up to the conductor's box.

The conductor was out of his box tending the stove. With a miniature shovel, he cleared the ashes from the bottom. Then he flipped open the little top door and added a shovelful of coal to the smouldering fire within. The coal dust ignited instantly in a shower of cheery red sparks. That chore done, he hopped back up on his perch to collect the fares and holler out the stops.

Dad had only one grown-up ticket and three children's. That meant Willa would have to scrunch down and pass for a kid. "If I'd known that I would have stayed at home," she grumbled under her breath.

"When the centre doors open," Dad whispered his instructions as we huddled around the stove, "you three skedaddle past the conductor and down the steps. I'll carry Jakey and put the tickets in all at once. That way he won't notice how big you are, Willa."

Poor Willa. She must have been six inches taller than the line on the pole that marked the difference between adults and children. But Dad's plan worked like a charm and he got transfers for all of us. Ten minutes later we boarded the Danforth car without a worry in the world.

It joggled and lurched along the tracks at a snail's pace (Arthur was sure he could run faster), and we finally arrived at Bathurst and Bloor. We always went that far along because it wasn't so crowded there. We hopped off not a minute too soon. Jakey's face had started to turn green.

Arthur and I squeezed onto the curb between two big boys who gave us dirty looks. Willa stood right behind us. Dad had no sooner hoisted Jakey onto his shoulders than he said, "I have to pee-pee, Daddy," so Dad told Willa to mind his place and he took Jakey down an alleyway. When they came back Jakey was all smiles, and the fresh air had brought the roses back to his cheeks.

The Mounties went prancing by, close enough to touch. Shivering with delight, we drew in our toes and stared up at the underside of their horses' big, round bellies.

At last came the faraway sound of music—beating drums and tooting horns and jingling tambourines. It was a wonderful parade. We saw Cinderella and the March Hare and Peter, Peter Pumpkin Eater. And in between came the upside-down clowns who patted our toques, and the swaying Humpty Dumpties who shook our mittens, and the glorious marching bands.

But the best was saved for last.

He stood high on a float in his make-believe sleigh, as high as the telephone poles. Santa Claus! The real one—not a helper or pretender. (Mum said only the real Santa was allowed to come to Toronto in Eaton's Santa Claus Parade.)

I held my breath as the mock reindeer drew nearer. (Mum

said Santa couldn't bring his live reindeer because Eaton's had nowhere to put them up.) Suddenly he was right beside us, "ho, ho, ho-ing" through his snowy beard, patting his round red stomach and throwing kisses to the four winds.

For a split second, the twinkling eyes met mine.

"Hello there, little Bluebird," he shouted down at me.

I gaped after him, my mouth hanging open, my eyes glued to his red velvet back.

"That was you Santa called Bluebird, Bea!" cried my astonished sister. "He noticed your new blue coat."

And then it was over. Only wisps of band music, like threads of smoke from a chimney, hung in the cold, damp air.

Already the crowds were surging towards the streetcars. Eager children were begging shivering parents to take them downtown to Eaton's department store to visit Santa in his Crystal Palace. Jakey was still grinning and waving from his perch on Dad's shoulders. Dad was wearing a big smile as if he had enjoyed the parade in spite of himself. The smile took me off guard.

"Can we go downtown to visit Santa, Dad?" I asked.

The smile dropped, like a mask, from his face. "No!" he barked, setting Jakey down with a thump. "We're going straight home. Write him a letter."

A lump rose painfully in my throat and my eyes swam with tears. But I knew better than to argue. I knew why Dad wouldn't take us to Eaton's. It wasn't because he was mean. Just the opposite. He was afraid we'd see some wonderful, expensive toy and ask Santa for it and be broken-hearted on Christmas morning when we didn't get it. But he needn't have worried, poor Dad. We understood that bicycles and doll sulkies, hobby

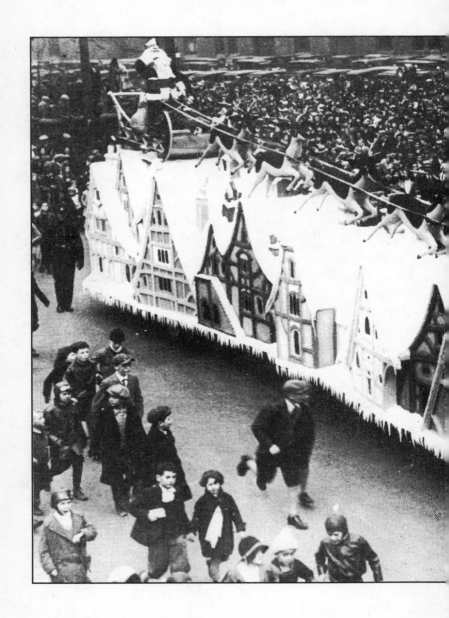

horses and Eaton Beauty dolls were not for the likes of us.

Willa noticed my face all crumpled up. "Maybe we could drop in on Aunt Maggie," she suggested. "She lives only a few blocks from here so it won't cost anything."

Dad's face brightened right up. "Good idea," he agreed. "Let's go." And he offered Jakey and me each a finger to hang on to.

My tears dried instantly at the mention of Aunt Mag. She was one of Mum's many sisters and a favourite of ours. She and Uncle Alistair lived in the heart of the city in a row house just like ours. Except they owned theirs and the bailiff could never put them out.

Uncle Alistair was an electrician. He belonged to the Electricians' Union and the Liberal Party. Mum said Uncle Alistair hadn't lost a single day's work on account of the Depression. That's what it was to have a good trade, she said. She often threw this up to Dad in the middle of a fight, so it's a wonder he was willing to go and visit them. But everybody liked Uncle Al, even Dad. There was a special bond between them. They had been comrades-in-arms in France from 1914 to 1918.

Aunt Maggie was well known in the family for always having the welcome mat out, and today was no exception. The door flew open at our knock.

"Come in, you're out!" she cried delightedly. "I was only half expecting you."

Her greetings were always little jokes like that. Willa said she had a quaint sense of humour.

"Well, Jim"—she turned her sunny smile on Dad—"and how's your old straw hat?"

Dad surprised us by returning her joke as he hung up his coat. "Pretty cold for it this time of year, Mag."

We followed her down the hall to the kitchen where Uncle Al sat with a tiny boy on his knee and a shy girl peeking round his elbow.

"Dear doctor," exclaimed Aunt Mag, ambling over to the stove in no particular hurry, "I've gone and burnt up the whole breakfast." Flipping the lid off the smoking saucepan with a long-handled spoon, she remarked matter-of-factly, "Burnt to a crisp. Oh well, once burnt, twice shy, I always say. We'll just have to make do with hen-fruit."

Tucking her hands under her armpits, she flapped her elbows and ran around the kitchen crowing "Cock-a-doodle-dooo!" like a chicken in a barnyard. We kids nearly split our sides laughing, and even Dad and Uncle Al had to smile.

Swooping down on the icebox, she took out a dozen eggs and cracked the whole works into a mixing bowl. Then she turned the gas jet high under the skillet and plopped in a big blob of real butter. Into the sizzling pan she poured the whole bowlful of eggs.

"Here, Willa." She handed my sister a long loaf of white bread. "You make the toasty-woasty for your Auntsy-Pantsy."

Arthur and I let out a whoop and even Willa smiled a bit as she began to slice the bread.

"You two straighten up," Dad warned us. Then to Aunt Mag, "You shouldn't be using your good food up on us, Mag. A cup of tea would have done just fine."

"Now you mind your beeswax, Jim Thomson," scolded our cheery aunt. "You just leave the 'brecky' to us chickens."

Arthur got the job of toastmaker and I was the official butterer.

We didn't have an electric toaster at our house so "toasty-woasty" was a special treat for us. The toaster fascinated Arthur. Its shiny sides lay open on the table. He put a slice of bread on each side and closed it up. At the exact right second, he flopped down the sides and the bread turned itself over automatically! When both sides were a lovely golden brown, he juggled them in the air and dropped them on a plate in front of me. The butter gave off a mouthwatering aroma as I spread it on the hot toast. It was all I could do not to take a bite.

What a swell breakfast that was: toast and jam and milk and tea and all the frizzled eggs we could eat. (And it wasn't even Easter!) We mopped our eggy plates with our crispy crusts until they shone. Then, without being asked, we helped Aunt Mag with the cleaning up. (Even Arthur asked for a dish towel!) While we worked she kept us laughing with her homey jokes and sunny disposition.

"It's time we were making tracks," Dad said when the dishes were done. "It wouldn't do to wear our welcome out."

"Fat chance!" retorted Aunt Mag. "You know you're as welcome as the flowers in May."

"Next time you come, Jim," said Uncle Alistair, "be sure you bring along that picture of you and me on leave in Paris."

"Will do," promised Dad. "Been nice talking to you."

It sure did Dad good to reminisce about the war.

"What do you say for all that good grub?" he reminded us in the pleasantest voice we'd heard in weeks.

"Thanks for all the good grub, Aunt Mag," we chorused.

As we went down the front walk she called after us, "Tell

Fran not to wait until a blue moon comes over the mountain—don't be strangers now. Orry-vor!"

We waved back and hollered, "Orry-vor!"

"What does orry-vor mean, Willa?" I asked, skippety-hopping beside her.

"She thinks she's saying *Au revoir*," explained my educated sister. "That's French for goodbye. But Aunt Mag never went to high school so she doesn't know how to pronounce it right."

Then and there I decided to go to high school and learn French. The way Willa said "*Au revoir*" was downright beautiful.

That night I took Dad's advice and wrote Santa a letter. I asked him for my heart's desire, a toy telephone. I had never used a real telephone, so I was dying to have one to practice on.

"Are you going to write to Santa this year?" I asked Willa.

"No, I haven't got time," she said, not looking up from her books. "You can put a p.s. on your letter and tell him I'd like a string of beads if he has any."

Importantly, I added her p.s.

"How about you, Arthur?" I was feeling very generous. "Want me to add a p.s. for you too?"

Arthur looked up from the map he was drawing. "Aw, I don't believe—oww!" He grabbed his leg under the table. Willa was staring at him fiercely. "I want a box of paints," he finished sullenly.

I had a good mind not to add his p.s., since he was so crabby about it, but I didn't want anything to spoil Christmas. I added some for Jakey and Billy too.

When I was finished I took another piece of paper and folded it into the shape of an envelope. Then I pasted it together with flour and water. Tucking my letter inside, I sealed it with a gooey white blob of paste.

"Can I have a stamp, Mum?" I asked.

"I haven't got one, Bea," she said, looking up from her mending. "If you put your letter on the hall table I'll remember to drop it in Santa's mailbox next time I'm down at Eaton's."

"Okay, Mum," I agreed happily. "No use wasting a stamp."

# 8

# A gloomy
# Christmas Eve

There was nothing to show it was the day before Christmas.
No last minute preparations, no whispered secrets, no delicious smell of bread and sage and onions coming from the big
mixing bowl.

The red and green crepe-paper streamers were still in the box
in the attic. The Christmas tree ornaments, little glass bells and
tiny red balls, were still packed in the shoe box in last year's
tissue paper.

Gloom hung like fog in the air. Mum and Dad had been fighting steadily for weeks, and now they weren't even speaking to
each other. I didn't know which was worse, the yelling or the
silence.

Usually on Christmas Eve Dad would go straight out after
supper to get our tree. He always left it that late on purpose so
he'd be sure to get a bargain. Then he generally got a tree for
a nickel.

I sat in the kitchen close to the stove remembering those
other years. How we'd all cluster around the front room window waiting with bated breath, watching for Dad to come
along with his peculiar, lopsided gait (caused by an improper-

ly set broken leg in childhood), dragging the tree behind him. It was nearly always a misshapen, scraggly old thing, but when Santa got finished trimming it, it was the most beautiful tree in the world. This year Dad didn't bother to go out because he didn't have two cents to rub together.

Willa was sitting on the opposite side of the stove mending her middy blouse. She sewed neat little stitches and when she was finished you could hardly see the patch. Mum had taught her to sew like that. I asked her to teach me too, but she said I was too much of a scatterbrain.

Arthur had his art pad out, drawing a reindeer drinking from a forest stream. I didn't know what to do with myself. I had no storybook to read and I was too down at the mouth to write a composition.

It was more like a funeral day than the day before Christmas. And to make matters worse the house was as cold as a barn, and we'd had to wear our coats all day.

The chair beside the kitchen stove was the warmest spot in the house, so I sat there and Mum gave me the baby to hold. He had colic and was crying. I sang "Rock-a-bye, baby," but instead of soothing him it made him cry even louder; so I swung him back and forth, faster and faster, in my arms. All of a sudden his head hit the stove with a wallop. Screwing up his skinny little face, he let out a bloodcurdling scream. Mum and Dad came running from opposite directions and Jakey squealed and dove under the table.

"Clumsy fool!" Dad bellowed, snatching the baby out of my arms.

I started to cry and couldn't stop even when Mum said it wasn't my fault and not to worry because Billy wasn't hurt.

At least the accident livened things up a bit. Dad and Mum started in fighting again. Willa and Arthur hightailed it up the stairs, and Jakey and I scurried down the cellar to play "Bill and Bob."

Bill and Bob was a rainy day game I had made up for Jakey. He'd ride his wobbly old kiddie car round and round the furnace and I'd be the friendly policeman. "Red light!" I'd say, holding up my hand. He'd come to a skidding stop, his dimples dancing. "Hi, Bill," I'd say. "How's everything at your house?" "Fine," he'd say, brown eyes sparkling. "How's your house?" "Fine," I'd say, bringing my hand down smartly. Then I'd say, "Green light!" and away he'd go, *brrmm, brrmm, brrmm* around the furnace. That's all there was to it. It wasn't much of a game but Jakey liked it better than London Bridge and Ring-Around-the-Rosy put together.

All we had for supper that night was potatoes and mashed turnips. Willa said. "Eww!" and left the table holding her nose. Dad gave her a baleful look. Arthur and I gobbled up her share. Jakey said he wanted bready milk instead, but there wasn't any milk so Dad made him up a bowl of bready water with brown sugar on it.

For the first time, that Christmas Eve, Willa and Arthur didn't hang up their stockings. When I went upstairs to hang Jakey's and mine on the bedposts, Willa followed me up. In a queer voice she said, "Bea, I don't think Santa is coming this year."

Then Arthur hollered from the bathroom, "There is no Santa Claus!" and ran into his bedroom slamming the door behind him.

"Liar! Liar! Ten feet higher!" I shrieked after him, tears

gushing down my face. "And you're mean, Willa, mean, mean, mean! Serves you right if Santa doesn't bring you anything!"

Then I changed my mind about where to hang our stockings. I decided to hang them on the knobs of a kitchen chair and put the chair right by the front door so Santa couldn't miss it when he came in.

"Don't forget to leave Santa a cup of hot cocoa," I reminded Mum as Jakey and I went to bed early. Jakey always slept with me on Christmas Eve because I had the spirit. Willa didn't care. She said it was a nice change to sleep by herself on the davenport. And Arthur was pleased as punch because for once he could be sure that no one would wet up his back.

Jakey cuddled up beside me, eyes snapping with excitement. "Bea-Bea, tell me stories," he said between thumb sucks.

So I recited "'Twas the night before Christmas" and I told him about old Ebenezer Scrooge, and about the baby Jesus being born in the manger in Bethlehem.

My eyes grew heavy and I nearly dropped off, but Jakey wouldn't let me. Lifting up one of my droopy eyelids, he whispered mysteriously, "BeaBea, are you still in there?"

I laughed so hard I was wide awake again, so I told him some more stories I made up out of my head. Then I ran him to the bathroom one more time and made him promise not to wet the bed or Willa would be mad.

# 9

# Arthur was right

Jakey was up like a shot at the crack of dawn. "Bea-Bea!" He shook me urgently. "I need to wee-wee!" For the first time in his life he hadn't wet the bed. So I ran him lickety-split to the bathroom.

Voices floated up the stairway. The teakettle was whistling, and I could hear Billy's hungry cry. Then I remembered what day it was and a sudden thrill went through me. Forgetting all about our dreary Christmas Eve, I yanked Jakey off the toilet and raced with him down the stairs.

Now there were two kitchen chairs sitting side by side at the front door. And four stockings with lumpy feet hung from the round wooden knobs.

Jakey let go of my hand and ran squealing to his stocking. Gleefully, he shook it upside down. Out onto the cracked linoleum rolled an apple, an orange and a little bag of candy. I dumped mine out beside his, and that's all there was in mine too—an apple, an orange and a little bag of candy.

There were no presents under the Christmas tree. There was no Christmas tree. No paintbox . . . no string of beads . . . no toy telephone. Just an apple, an orange and a handful of hard candies in a twist of waxed paper.

"Mum," I said, looking up from the cold floor into her troubled eyes, "did you mail my letter?"

"Yes, Booky," she said.

So Arthur was right. There was no Santa Claus. My eyes were so full of tears I could hardly see the belly button on my orange.

Willa sat on the edge of the davenport wrapped in a quilt. Her brown freckles stood out like black pepper spilled on a white tablecloth. She didn't make a move, so Mum handed her her stocking.

"Here, Willa," she said. "Have your orange for breakfast." Willa took the stocking but she didn't dump it out.

By ten o'clock our treats were all gone, even though we tried to drag them out.

"Let's play Bill and Bob, Bea-Bea," said Jakey. But I didn't feel like it. There was a big lump in my chest.

Willa went upstairs to make the beds. Arthur was putting the finishing touches on his picture. Jakey was under the table sucking his thumb and Billy had dropped off to sleep. I could hear Dad in the cellar furiously sifting ashes. Mum was banging pots and pans in the kitchen. I couldn't remember ever feeling so sad before. My chest ached and I couldn't breathe right.

A sudden knock on the front door made us all jump out of our skins.

"Land sakes!" Mum exclaimed. "Who could that be?"

The knock brought Dad up from the cellar. Jakey came out from his hiding place, Willa came halfway down the stairs, and Arthur and I followed Mum to the door.

A strange man stood on the rickety porch with four long boxes on his arm. "Merry Christmas from the Star Santa Claus Fund," he cried in a put-on merry voice. Then he tipped his hat and left.

On top of each box was a Santa Claus sticker with a message printed on it. *Boy, 10–12, Girl, 8–10, Boy, 3–5,* and one that just said *Baby boy.*

The weight on my chest shifted a little. "Can we open them, Mum?" I said.

"Sure, Bea. It's Christmas."

Each Star box contained clothing, a toy and a candy cane. Out of the *Girl, 8–10* box I pulled a long black sweater-coat and matching toque. Both were trimmed with a double orange stripe. My toy was a Betty-Boop doll with huge painted eyes looking over to one side, black-painted hair and fat stuck-together legs.

Arthur got the same toque and sweater, but his buttoned on the other side. His toy was a Snakes and Ladders game. Jakey got a blue sweater and toque and a picture book. Billy got a blue layette and a rattle. Willa didn't get a box because she was too big. She said she was glad because she hated the black toque and sweater. Dad told her to hold her tongue, so she didn't say boo for hours.

The first thing I did was change Betty-Boop's name to Lucy after "Lucy in the Lighthouse." That was one of my favourite stories in the Junior Third Reader. Whenever I couldn't sleep at night for Billy crying or Mum and Dad fighting or Willa snoring, I'd imagine I was Lucy struggling up the spiral staircase with the heavy lantern. Breathlessly I'd hang it in the narrow lighthouse window so its wavering light could be seen far out to sea. It was thrilling to be a heroine and save all those sailor boys from certain death on the rocky reefs below.

Willa did a real nice thing for me that day. She made Lucy a cute little dress out of a blue-checkered scrap from Mum's rag bag. She said she would have made bloomers too if Lucy's legs hadn't been stuck together.

Usually our Aunt Aggie in Muskoka sent us a chicken for Christmas, but this year there wasn't one. Instead Mum made a big pot of potato soup for our noonday meal. It wasn't much, but it was delicious: thick and hot with onions swimming in it and parsley floating on the top. I could have eaten a whole barrelful, easy. But there was only enough for one bowl each.

As she stacked the bowls, Mum started in grumbling. Then Dad said a swear word and stomped off down the cellar. I was just about to follow him when another knock came at the door.

"Land sakes!" Mum declared again, and I followed her instead.

Mr. Westover stood on the porch. He looked embarrassed. Gawking past him I could see Audrey in her fur-trimmed coat sitting on her mother's lap in the Model A Ford. I waved and she waved back with her fur muff.

Mr. Westover handed Mum a brown parcel. "Merry Christmas, Mrs. Thomson," he said and quickly walked away before Mum had a chance to say, "Same to you."

Curiosity had brought Dad back up the stairs. We all gathered round the dining room table to watch Mum open the parcel. In it was a roast of pork, two tins of ungraded peas, a red jelly powder and a storebought Christmas cake.

Dad scowled at the little pile of groceries. "We don't need their charity!" he snarled.

"Oh, yes, we do!" Mum barked back.

Then she started to scold in earnest. I guess she just couldn't help herself, even on Christmas. All her worries and heartaches came tumbling out together: the rent was overdue and the bailiff was after us again; there was no food in the cabinet; we all had holes in our shoes; the baby needed a doctor, and Willa needed books to study from. On and on she went, all afternoon.

Dad sat as still as a statue. His face was the colour of dry cement. Long before he exploded, my legs had begun to shake.

His anger burst out in a torrent of rage and the swear words he used were something wicked. Mum just hurled them back in his face. Dreadful, hateful, evil words flew back and forth across the room like lightning bolts in a thunderstorm.

I don't know what she said to make him hit her. All I remember was the terrible sound, like a clap of thunder. A piercing scream pealed from her throat, scaring the wits out of us kids. Willa ran coatless out the door, Arthur bolted up the stairs, Billy howled, and Jakey darted out from under the table, bit Dad on the leg and dove for cover again. I clung to the table's edge, my legs wobbling like jelly, and screamed for them to stop. But they didn't even hear me.

At last Dad grabbed his greatcoat from the cellar door and went slamming out of the house. I slid down on the chair beside Mum. My stomach was churning, my head was paining, and my eyes had gone all blurry. I could hear Mum's breath coming in quick little gasps. Her face was beet-red and streaked with tears.

Willa came back, blue from the cold, and went upstairs without speaking. Arthur didn't come down. Jakey crept out from under the table and laid his curly head on Mum's lap. His eyes were big as saucers.

"C'mon, Jakey," I whispered. "Let's go down to the cellar and play Bill and Bob."

By the time Mum called us up for supper, my stomach was cleaving to my backbone. The table was set in the kitchen, which was strange for Christmas Day. We always ate in the dining room on special occasions.

The roast pork looked delicious, all crisp and brown, with a bowl of golden gravy right beside it. Dad walked in in the middle of the meal. He looked neither to left nor to right. He hung up his greatcoat on the cellar door and sat down at his place. His face wasn't grey anymore. Now it was red from the cold. Mum's cheeks had changed from bright red to a pale yellow. There were purple bruises on one side.

We ate in silence, passing the food around. I loaded up my plate with thick, juicy pork, sweet green peas and fluffy mashed potatoes swimming in rich brown gravy. It was so good, my headache went away.

For dessert, Mum served up the store-bought fruitcake with a cup of weak tea for each of us. There was no milk. We cleaned up every crumb of cake. Mum had a thick slice herself, but Dad wouldn't touch it.

I felt so much better after eating that I jumped up to help Willa with the dishes. She gave me a queer look but didn't say anything. Then, while Mum was bathing the baby and Dad was putting Jakey to bed, Arthur said to Willa, "Do you want a game of Snakes and Ladders?" I said, "Can three play?" and

Arthur said, "Sure," just as nice as you please.

We played for a couple of hours on the kitchen table and Arthur and I didn't even fight once. I guess we had had enough of fighting for one day. Especially Christmas Day.

I was glad when it was time for bed. I went up early to be alone for a while. Snuggling under the thin covers with Lucy hard against my cheek, I thought the day over. I understood now why Willa and Arthur had said what they did about Santa. They weren't being mean. They were just trying to save me from being disappointed.

All of a sudden I stopped feeling sorry for myself and started feeling sorry for my parents. I realized the heart-aches they suffered and the shame they felt in front of people like the Westovers and the Star Santa Claus man.

I thought about Audrey and what her Christmas had been like. I knew she had got her fur-trimmed coat because I had caught a glimpse of it that morning. Last year Santa had brought

20 ins. Tall

**Just a Great Big Armful of Value! 1 00**

**618-607** She's one of Santa's favorites—Miss **"EATON Beauty."** Mother knows she is such good value and little daughter is fascinated by her long curls, her sweet smile, sleeping eyes, real lashes and moving bisque head. Composition body, fully jointed at head, shoulders, elbows, wrists, legs and knees. Removable shoes, socks and lace-trimmed slip. All ready to be dressed! Size 20 ins. high.. **1.00**
**618-625.** Head only to fit above doll.... **39c**
**618-626.** Wig only...... **50c**

her an Eaton Beauty doll. Then they had gone to her grandmother's for turkey dinner.

I thought of something else too, something that had lain heavy on my heart for many weeks now. I wondered if it was the Westovers who had wanted to adopt our Billy. That's how they got Audrey, and they still had an empty bedroom. No, it couldn't have been them because I remembered how surprised Mrs. Westover had been when I told her about Billy being born. But it was probably somebody like them, somebody rich and kind and good, who could have given Billy wonderful Christmases so he wouldn't have to find out about Santa Claus too soon.

Deep down in my heart I had never forgiven my mother for wanting to give Billy away. I had been on my father's side of that argument. But now I understood how Mum, who loved her children as fiercely as a tiger, could actually consider giving one of us up. If Billy had lots of milk and a warm cot and parents who didn't fight all the time, he probably wouldn't cry at all. Poor baby.

And poor Mum too.

Just before I fell asleep I remembered something else. There had been no empty cocoa cup on the kitchen table that morning.

"For sure there is no Santa Claus, Lucy," I whispered, choking back a sob, my tears spilling on her black celluloid hair. "And I don't care! But oh, how I missed our Christmas tree!"

# 10

# Hiding from the bailiff

1933 got off to a noisy start at midnight with everyone in the neighbourhood standing knee-deep in the snow, blowing horns and whistles, banging pots and pans together and hollering "Happy New Year!" to one another. 1932 had been such a bad year we were all glad to see the last of it.

The celebrating was fun while it lasted, but it was over in no time and there was nothing left to do but go back to bed again.

On New Year's Day two lovely things happened that almost made up for Christmas. First, the postman brought Aunt Aggie's chicken. (*Merry Xmas! Better late than never*, read the soggy note tied to the chicken's leg.) And then Dave and Mary Atlas arrived all the way from Saskatoon, Saskatchewan. They were staying downtown at the "King Eddie" and they took a taxicab right to our door. Imagine!

They had "neither chick nor child" themselves, so they made a big fuss over us kids. Mary especially loved our Arthur. She would!

Dave was a barrel of fun. He had been Mum's beau when they were young. So he liked to tease us by saying that if Mum had married him he'd be our father instead of Dad.

As soon as they left that night, with lots of kissing and hugging at the door, Dad went straight down to the cellar. So I followed him. There was something I wanted to know.

"Dad . . ."

He glanced up and I noticed that his eyes were as blue as Billy's.

"Is that true what Dave said?"

"Is what true?"

"That if Mum had married him he'd be our father?"

"No," he answered shortly. "He was only joshing. If you weren't my children you wouldn't be here at all."

Standing on tiptoe, I planted a peck on his sharp-boned cheek. "I'm glad, Dad," I said.

He looked at me sort of surprised. "Get away with you," he said gently. Then he started sifting ashes.

A few days later it was washday, which meant it was Monday. Mum never washed any other day. Sometimes, if she wasn't feeling well, I'd say, "Why don't you wash tomorrow, Mum?" But she'd say no, the wash had to be done on Monday—and the ironing had to be done on Tuesday. It was the same with all her work. The floors had to be scrubbed on Friday and she had to bake on Saturday, just as religiously as we had to go to church on Sunday. That's the way she was.

Mum was tired right out from scrubbing on the washboard all morning long, then lugging the heavy basket up the cellar stairs to hang the clothes on the backyard line. She wasn't a strong woman, my mum. She'd had rheumatic fever when she was a little girl and it left her with a weak heart. So scrubbing on the board for seven people nearly wore her to a frazzle.

About twice a year she managed to get the use of an electric

washing machine. She'd order it "on trial" from Eaton's for thirty days and two dollars deposit. Then when the thirty days were up she'd write Eaton's a letter saying she didn't like the machine and would they please send their horse and wagon out to pick it up. The driver and his helper would lug the heavy appliance up from the cellar, load it on the delivery wagon, and then politely give Mum her money back. Everybody on "pogey" did that. They'd wash everything in sight for a whole month and then swear by all that's good and holy that they weren't satisfied with the washing machine. Of course Eaton's knew what they were up to. But what could they do? Timothy Eaton had promised "Goods satisfactory or money refunded."

On this particular washday Mum didn't have a machine, so she was tired and crabby. I was the only one home for dinner that day. Willa took her lunch to high school, so she was gone all day, and Arthur didn't come home because he got a free meal in the school basement. Every day it was served up to all the poor kids. Except me. I had been expelled from the free meal program.

Right after my last free meal I had been sitting on the school steps telling Audrey all about it—how the chicken soup had no chicken in it, and the sandwiches had no butter on them, and the blancmange tasted like wallpaper paste. (Actually I was just being a smart aleck. I had really enjoyed the whole dinner.) Suddenly a big hand reached down and grabbed me by the shoulder. Unbeknownst to me, Mrs. Rice, the school principal, had been standing behind us on the top step and had heard every word I said. She was a big, strong, strict woman (one of the few women principals in York County) and she dragged me down the hall to her office just like a rag doll. The vice-principal leaped to attention as we entered. For a minute I thought he was going to salute.

"Mr. Lord," boomed Old-Lady-Rice-Pudding in a voice that sounded like thunder, "what do you think of an ungrateful girl who was distinctly heard to criticize the free meal program for the poor?"

I could feel both pairs of righteous eyes boring down on me. My legs had begun to wobble, so I grabbed the desk for support.

"I think said girl should be expelled from said program," said Mr. Lord.

"I wholeheartedly agree. I shall write a letter at once to her parents."

When the stone-faced principal handed me a long white envelope, licked and sealed and addressed to both my parents, I knew for sure I was "said girl."

"Beatrice"—now her voice was like a preacher's at a funeral—"deliver this envelope to your mother and father with the seal unbroken and return it to me tomorrow morning bearing both their signatures."

The plan being born in my mind died with her last words. I had pictured myself happily ripping the letter into shreds and letting it flutter like confetti out onto Kingston Road. Then all I would have to do was go without dinner for the rest of the year and nobody would be the wiser.

Mum's dark-winged eyebrows knitted together as she read it, and her forehead creased in a frown. "Oh, pshaw, Bea," she said worriedly, "you need that good meal to put some meat on your bones."

"No, I don't, Mum. Honest. And anyway I still get the free

milk at recess. The school nurse says I have to have it until I'm only nineteen pounds underweight instead of twenty."

"Well, just the same, you could really do with that dinner. What did Mrs. Rice hear you say?"

"I was just telling Audrey that the blancmange tasted like wallpaper paste. And it did, Mum. It wasn't nice and creamy like yours."

I knew she hated to do it, but after supper she showed the letter to Dad. The colour drained from his face as he read. Without a word he took me by the scruff of my neck and dragged me up the stairs. Reaching for the razor-strop off the bathroom door, he ordered me to pull my bloomers down. I screamed bloody murder before even one blow had landed on my bare behind.

Up the stairs, her cheeks flaming, raced my little mother. Grabbing the strop out of Dad's hand in midair, she shrieked at him, "Leave her alone! It's a free country, you know! Bea's got a right to her opinion!"

I never knew that before! It was my first lesson in democracy. And it must have made some sense to Dad too, because he hung the strop back up and never so much as mentioned the incident again.

As it turned out, Mrs. Rice had done me a big favour. My mother's never-to-be-forgotten words were to ring in my heart for the rest of my life. And ever after that, when I had a fight with Willa or Arthur, I always got the last word by screaming at the top of my lungs, "It's a free country, you know! I've got a right to my opinion!" I nearly drove them crazy.

So that's how come I was the only one home at noon that day. The second I set foot on the back porch, the door flew open and Mum's hand shot out and yanked me inside.

"What's the matter, Mum?" I asked anxiously as she locked the door behind me.

"It's Ratman. He's across the road."

The bailiff's dreaded name made cold duck-bumps pop out all over my skinny body. He had been hounding us unmercifully ever since we'd come to Birchcliff. Three times in the past year he had tried to serve us with eviction papers, and three times we had foiled him by pretending we were out.

Oh, how I hated that man! I used to pray he would drop dead on the sidewalk so we wouldn't have to worry any more about being put out on the street with our furniture. Of course, it never occurred to me that he was only doing his job, and that if he didn't do it somebody else would.

Running to the front window, I peered fearfully through the frayed, starched curtains. He was crossing the street and was near enough for me to see his beady little eyes and rat-like nose.

"Here he comes, Mum!"

Quick as a wink she herded Jakey and me, with Billy in her arms, up the stairs to her bedroom. "Let's pretend we're playing hide-and-seek and Mr. Ratman is 'it,'" she said, trying to make a game of it for Jakey's sake.

But even the little three-year-old wasn't fooled. He wriggled under the bed with me, his eyes as big and black as agates. I held him tight and felt his heart pounding wildly like my own. Billy started to fuss. Then he gave a loud suck as Mum stuffed the dummy in. She jiggled him on the edge of the bed. I could see the curve of her calves under the skimpy counterpane. She had nice legs, my Mum.

The first loud bang on the door scared the daylights out of us. Jakey's little body jerked convulsively and his eyes nearly popped out of his head. I squeezed him tighter, my heart flopping painfully. Billy tried to cry and Mum jiggled faster, making the bedsprings squeak overhead.

The hammering went on and on. *Bang! Bang! Bang! Thump! Thump! Thump!* Then a loud crack that sounded like a kick. Boy, he was stubborn, that Ratman. I thought he'd never give up. But at long last we heard his footsteps creaking down the wooden steps.

"Be still a while longer," Mum said quietly. "He might be back."

We stayed stock-still. Jakey was as good as gold and didn't make a peep.

At last Mum stood up and the bedsprings rose above us. "He's gone," she said, loosening her hold on the dummy. The second the plug was out Billy let loose with a howl that could probably be heard all the way up to Audrey's.

As soon as Dad came in the door she started in on him. "I'm sick and tired of hiding from the bailiff and scaring the living daylights out of these children," she fumed bitterly. "And for two cents I'd go out and get a job myself."

That made Dad boil, because in those days a man would have to be a cripple in a wheelchair before he'd let his wife go out to work. So what followed was their biggest fight ever.

Talk about scared! Jakey dove under the table, Arthur made a beeline down the cellar, and Willa high-tailed it out the back door without her coat again. I just clung to the back of a chair and shook.

# 11

# Our brand new house

Two weeks later the bailiff caught us red-handed. Another big fight was in full swing when there came a loud banging on the door. With all that racket going on, there was no use pretending we were out.

Dad flung the door open angrily, and there stood Ratman on the porch. His face was long and sad like a hound dog's. Close up he didn't look like a rat at all.

"I'm sorry, sir," he said, tipping his hat, "but you have two weeks to get out." He handed Dad an official looking paper, tipped his hat again, and left. Hearing him say he was sorry took me by surprise.

The next day Mum and Dad started house-hunting again. One good thing, there were lots of empty houses to choose from. People were always on the move for one reason or another. The few that owned their own homes lost them because they couldn't pay the mortgage. And the rest of us got put out on the street because we couldn't pay the rent.

My biggest worry was that we might have to move to the wrong side of the tracks. Or even worse, downtown to Cabbagetown. Mum said that's where the real down-andouters ended up. The ones who had lost their pride.

Dad always house-hunted in those grubby old districts. But he might just as well have saved his energy because Mum wouldn't even look at the places he found. She said children had to be raised in a good neighbourhood. She said environment was important. Dad said environment was hogwash. He said if parents were strict enough and set a good example their kids would turn out right as rain no matter where they were brought up.

Sure enough, home he came with a latchkey from a house on the wrong side of the tracks. I nearly had a fit. What would Audrey say? But before I had time to get upset about it Mum came home with a latchkey from a house on the right side. The only trouble was the rent for Mum's house was six dollars a month. The rent for Dad's was only four.

"Two dollars a month will buy a lot of bread," Dad said glumly.

I had to admit he was right. There was a store on Kingston Road that sold leftover Saturday bread on Monday mornings for five cents a loaf. Even I could figure out how much bread two dollars would buy, if I put my mind to it.

But Mum wouldn't budge. She said her house was in a respectable neighbourhood, far from the railroad tracks and sooty trains and hobos. She said it would be well worth the extra money, and she quoted the Bible to back her up. "Man cannot live by bread alone," she said.

Dad never argued with the Bible.

But right or wrong side of town, the houses we moved to always seemed to have one thing in common. They were full of dirt and bedbugs. People were terrible in those days for

leaving their dirt behind them. Dad said it was their way of getting back at the all-powerful landlord. But Mum said it showed a lack of pride and breeding. "No one will ever say that Frances Cole Thomson was brought up in a pigsty," she'd breathlessly declare as she wore her fingers to the bone scouring the house we were leaving. Then she'd turn around and do the same thing to the one we were moving into.

Bedbugs were by far the worst problem. The pesky little devils with their nut-brown shells were almost impossible to kill. Poor Mum would drive herself nearly crazy until the last one was squashed. I remember one time when the filthy vermin (as Mum called them) got into the baby's cot and bit his bottom to pieces. Dad had to take his cot out in the backyard and burn the mattress and pour boiling water down the hollow iron posts before he finally got rid of them. But it was a losing battle just the same. No sooner had you got rid of yours than you caught a new batch from your neighbour. Most people just learned to live with them, like flies in summertime.

But on this particular move we had a marvellous stroke of luck. Right in the middle of the battle of the latchkeys, Willa came home and casually mentioned that there was a brand new house for rent on Cornflower Street. Cornflower Street was just a block south of Lilac, so Mum dragged Dad down to see it, with him complaining all the way. And they got it. For six dollars a month. A brand new house!

There wasn't a speck of dirt or a bedbug to be seen. All Mum had to do was sweep up some nice-smelling wood shavings and scrape up a blob of snow-white plaster off the hardwood floor. Our old furniture never looked so beautiful and never gleamed so lemon-oil bright as it did in its own reflection on those oaken hardwood floors.

Mum was practically beside herself with joy. She went about whistling like a robin in a loaded cherry tree. That's what she did when she was happy. She whistled while she worked, and it was music to our ears.

In our wildest dreams we'd never hoped to live in such a house. It had a big bay window and a wide hardwood staircase with a smooth oak banister that was just perfect for sliding down when nobody was looking.

And it had storm windows to keep out the cold, and a fenced-in yard for Jakey and Billy. And it even had an upstairs verandah, right on top of the downstairs one. We could hardly wait for summertime to take the kitchen chairs out to sit on it.

The cellar had closed-in steps you couldn't fall through, and a shiny new furnace and a real cement floor. Just perfect for playing Bill and Bob in. The cellar floor in the old house had been dank, dark, hard-packed clay.

And the bathroom! The fixtures were all gleaming white and the water closet was right behind the toilet, instead of over-head with a chain hanging down. You could flush it with just a flick of your finger. And best of all, hot water came right out of the tap. So Dad wouldn't have to lug boilerfuls of scalding water up two flights of stairs any more

It would take years, I thought, to get used to all the luxuries in the new house. But I didn't need to worry my head about that. Not even one year went by before the bailiff was back at our door.

# 12

# A visit with Grampa

"'Tis cauld agine!" cried Mum, as she jumped back inside the door after shaking out her cedar mop.

"Who used to say that, Mum?" asked Willa. We were always curious about those funny old sayings from long ago.

"Old Mr. Levis," laughed Mum. "He used to come to our back door twice a week with the groceries, and all winter long he'd greet my mother with the exact same words. 'Tis cauld agine, Mrs. Cole!"

"What does it mean, Mum?" asked Arthur.

"It just means it's cold again," explained Mum.

The cold weather showed no sign of letting up. It was the coldest March we could remember.

On Saturday we kids stayed in all day. Jakey and I spent most of the time in the cellar playing Bill and Bob. After supper he wanted to play some more, but I was tired of it so I got the photograph album out to distract him.

"Who's that, Bea-Bea?" He pointed with a chubby finger at a faded snapshot of two young women, one small and neat and pretty, the other fat and sloppy and homely as a hedge fence.

74

Pointing to the pretty one, I said, "That's Mum when she was young. Who's that with you, Mum?"

She leaned on the broom handle and glanced over my shoulder. "Oh, that's my old chum, Beulah Haggett. She was a barrel of fun and a sight for sore eyes. She came to a bad end, Beulah did. But it wasn't her fault, poor thing, it was the way she was brought up. Puppa said old man Haggett was as crooked as a dog's hind leg, and Mumma said he was so mean he'd steal the pennies off a dead man's eyes. Their house was as filthy as a pigsty too, and they had so many children they had to eat in relays. I remember one time I stayed for supper and Beulah and I had to wait for the second sitting. Well, dashed if her mother didn't dish up the stew on the same plates the others had just eaten off. I tell you, it nearly made me gag."

Jakey and I squealed with laughter at the story and Willa wiggled her nose and said "Eww!"

Mum continued reminiscing. "They had the most cunning baby in their family. His name was Herbie and that little urchin wouldn't drink anything but tea. Well, one day Beulah put milk in his bottle by mistake and the young whelp took one gulp and threw the bottle across the floor, bellyragging at the top of his lungs, 'Who put milk in my tea-baw?' Tea! Imagine! No wonder the little imp's milk teeth all came in the colour of mud."

"What's that thing on your arm, Mum?" Jakey was pointing to a black band on her coat sleeve in the picture.

"That's a mourning band," she answered quietly, "for my mother when she died. I wore it for a whole year. People don't do that so much any more."

She took the album in her hands and turned the page. Softly her chapped red fingers caressed the photo of a woman with sunken cheeks and sad eyes and dark hair drawn back in a bun. "There's Mumma," she murmured. Then she went back to her work.

The next morning, Sunday, at the breakfast table Mum said, "I have to see Puppa today."

"You picked a fine day for it," grumbled Dad. "It must be ten below out there." He had just come back in from scraping off the porch steps with the coal shovel.

But Mum's mind was made up, so off we set right after our noonday meal, Mum and Dad, Jakey, Billy and me. Arthur and Willa had to stay home because they weren't all better yet from having their tonsils out on the kitchen table.

That had happened the week before. Jakey and I had been making a snowman in the yard and I had to go to the bathroom. When I started in the back door Mum blocked my way and said in a nervous voice, "You can't come in until I call you." I said, "But I have to go bad, Mum," and she said, "Well, you'll just have to hold it," and shut the door in my face.

By the time she called us in I could hardly walk and I had a terrible pain in my stomach.

Coming inside from the fresh air, I noticed a funny mediciney smell in the kitchen. There were red drops on the linoleum around the table legs.

I ran upstairs to the bathroom and when I came out, my stomach easing with relief, I saw Willa and Arthur in their beds—and it wasn't even suppertime. They were both white as ghosts. Willa was asleep with her mouth open. Brown stuff dribbled from the corners. Arthur was crying pitifully.

He had a stained bib around his neck.

Hurrying downstairs, I asked anxiously, "What's the matter with Willa and Arthur, Mum?"

"Dr. Hopkins took their tonsils out," she said, scrubbing the red spots off the linoleum. "Take Jakey down the cellar to play so there won't be any noise. They need their rest."

"Will I have to have my tonsils out too, Mum?"

"Not right now anyway, Booky. Away you go like a good girl while I get the supper on."

So that's how come there were only five of us struggling down Kingston Road against the cold west wind on that Sunday afternoon.

At the city limits we clambered up the high steps of the red, wooden streetcar and hurried down to the stove beside the conductor's box. Huddling around it, we held out frost-bitten fingers to catch its rosy glow.

Two and a half hours later we disembarked in Swansea. Then came the long, cold walk down Windermere Avenue to the cement-block house that Grampa had built.

"Well, this is a surprise!" he beamed, opening the door wide. "I didn't expect anybody on a day like this."

You could tell he was happy to see us, but Evie and Joey, his two youngest children, gave us dark, baleful looks. Not much wonder, because the minute Mum set eyes on them she ordered them upstairs to wash themselves. She acted more like their mother than their sister, which wasn't surprising because they weren't much older than Willa and Arthur.

Grampa always got a big kick out of Jakey. (I guess that's because Jakey was a Cole. The rest of us kids were dyed-in-the-wool Thomson.) He ruffled Jakey's curls and laughed out loud when the little fellow cried, "Have a drink, Grampa, so the drips will fall off your moustache."

Obligingly Grampa took a swig from a murky glass and waggled his head to make the water fly. Squealing with delight, Jakey danced around catching the silver droplets in midair.

This attention to my little brother never made me jealous because Grampa and I, ever since I could remember, had had an understanding. He said we were kindred spirits.

Mum set about the work she had come to do, sweeping and baking and putting up a nice hot supper. Dad walked the baby around the big old house. Billy knew he was in a strange place and his wide blue eyes stared curiously over Dad's shoulder, taking everything in.

Evie was mad because Willa hadn't come. She couldn't be bothered with me. She was a pretty girl with large violet eyes and naturally curly chestnut hair.

"You look more like Mumma every day, Evie," Mum said. "You're pretty as a picture."

The compliment cheered Evie right up and she began to play the Victrola. Lifting the square walnut lid, she searched in the steel cup for a sharp needle. Then she put a record on and cranked the handle on the side of the big box, and out of the horn-shaped speaker came a man's voice singing through his nose. Inside the lid was a picture of a little dog cocking its head as if the singing hurt its ears. When the music slowed down, Evie cranked it up again. She did that all afternoon.

Joey had put on his cap and windbreaker and gone out the minute we arrived. He usually played with Arthur.

Jakey had settled himself on the davenport with the stereoscope. The eyepiece fit snugly around the eyes, blocking out the light like blinders on a horse. A double picture fitted into a slot at the end of a long stick. You slid the picture up and down the stick until it came into focus. Then Niagara Falls and the Rocky Mountains and the animals at Riverdale Zoo stood out large as life in three dimensions.

While everybody was busy doing all these things, I just followed Grampa around. When he was finished with his chores, he sat down beside the kitchen stove and lit his corncob pipe.

"Can I comb your hair, Grampa?" I asked, patting the thick grey bristles.

"If you like, Be-*a*-trice." He was the only person who pronounced my name that way. I liked it from him, but if anybody else had said it I would have had a conniption fit.

The minute I started fussing with his hair he closed his eyes and sucked on his pipe, making a soft, contented *putt-putt* sound. While I combed, I talked a blue streak, telling him everything that came into my head. He answered with a quiet murmur to let me know he was listening.

"It's time you had a trim, Grampa," I said.

"Mmm," he said without opening his eyes.

The scissors hung on a nail on the side of the cupboard. Mum handed them to me without a word.

I chattered and clipped, the steel-grey hair crunching between the blades and falling, like bits of silver wire, onto his stooped plaid shoulders.

"Hold still now, Grampa," I ordered, "while I trim the tea off your moustache." He pursed his lips, trying not to smile, the pipe clenched between his teeth.

It was then I noticed the deep-cut lines on either side of his mouth. I stopped trimming and looked closer at his weather-beaten face. His forehead was heavily furrowed, like a fresh-ploughed field, and fine lines zig-zagged all over his high olive cheekbones.

The faded brown eyes flickered open. He took the corncob from his mouth. "Are you done already, Be-*a*-trice?"

"No, Grampa, but I'm worried about something."

"What might that be?"

"Are you old, Grampa?"

"Old beside you, I reckon."

"Was Grandma old when she died?"

"No. She never lived to be old."

"Don't die Grampa!" The words burst out in a tortured sob and I flung my arms around his neck.

I heard Mum gasp, then I felt my grandfather's strong arms around me. "Don't you worry none about that, Be-*a*-trice," he said, patting my back. "When I go, I won't go far. I'll just set myself down and light my pipe and wait outside the gates. I won't go in without you."

"Really, Grampa? You're not just saying that."

"Cross my heart and spit," he said.

And he did. He crossed his heart, then lifted the iron stove lid and spat a long sizzling stream into the crackling fire. That made me laugh like anything. He only lived three more years after that, but his love for me has lasted all my life.

We left for home right after supper. The temperature had dropped another five degrees.

"It's not a fit night for man nor beast," grumbled Dad.

It was pure torture leaving the cosy streetcar at the city limits. Poor little Jakey had gone fast asleep beside the stove.

What a shock he got to find himself plunked on his feet on the sidewalk in the freezing cold.

Chill winds gusted across the golf links. Dad strode ahead, acting as a windbreak, with Billy tucked deep inside his great-coat. I staggered after him, clinging to his coattails. Mum brought up the rear, half dragging and half carrying my tear-ful little brother.

The low-burning fire in the shiny furnace of the new house never felt so good and never welcomed us so warmly as it did on that below zero night when we came home from Grampa's.

# 13

# The Annex

April came at last, but spring didn't come with it. There was still lots of snow on the ground. My galoshes were all worn out so I had stopped wearing them. My shoes were holey and leaked like sieves. Dad had half-soled them twice already but there was no use doing it again because the toes were scuffed out and my brown ribbed stockings showed through.

One morning I came home from Sunday School and went in the back way so as not to make tracks on the hardwood. A big snowdrift leaned against the porch. Mum had a bowl of red jelly setting in it. It looked pretty nested in the white snow. I tested it with my finger. Mmm, raspberry. It wasn't quite set. I licked my finger and went in.

Mum was leaning over the kitchen table, her chin cupped in her hands, reading Saturday's newspaper. Every day the Armstrongs, who lived next door to the new house, gave us yesterday's copy of the *Evening Telegram*. Then on Sundays they gave us the Saturday *Star Weekly*.

Mum read the paper from front to back. Dad didn't bother with it except to read "Uncle Wiggley" to Jakey. He said the news made him sick. Arthur and I always fought over the comics, especially the coloured ones in the *Star Weekly*. His favourite was "The Katzenjammer Kids." Mine was "Bringing Up Father" (I loved how Maggie bounced that rolling pin off old Jiggs's head). Willa liked "Ella Cinders" and "Tillie the Toiler," but she wouldn't fight over it. She'd just wait her turn.

I showed Mum my shoes and she exclaimed, "My stars, Bea, where are your galoshes?"

"They're all wore out, Mum," I said.

"Well, you can't go to school like that. You'd better stay home tomorrow and we'll take a run downtown. Monday is Opportunity Day at Eaton's."

My heart skipped at the prospect. There was nothing in the world I'd rather do than go downtown with my mother. And on a school day too!

Dad stayed home to mind the little ones. It made a nice change for him, not having to go out looking for work.

We walked to the city limits as usual, but this time we didn't mind because spring was in the air.

"We'll go the long way round and drop in on Susan," Mum said, a lilt in her voice. It did her a world of good to get out of the house.

My Aunt Susan was a real live store lady. The name of her store was The Uptown Nuthouse. We kids just loved making jokes about visiting the nuthouse.

When Aunt Susan first opened her store, right in the middle of the Depression, everybody said she'd never make a go of it. "What does a woman know about running a business anyway?" they said, and, "Who's going to waste money on confections in these hard times?" But Aunt Susan just ignored them, and her nut and candy business flourished.

She roasted the nuts herself in a big pot of boiling oil right in the little shop window for everyone to see. And smell! Winter and summer the shop door stood wide open and the tantalizing aroma of roasting cashews drifted deliciously all over the four corners of Toronto's main intersection. Practically everybody who stepped off the streetcars at Yonge and Bloor, no matter what direction they were going, automatically followed their noses into my Aunt Susan's store.

Sometimes Aunt Milly worked there too. She was Mum's fourth-to-the-youngest sister. We could see her now, handing out free samples on the sidewalk. "Step right up, folks. Get 'em while they're hot," she called out gaily. "Fresh roasted cashews, ready or not!"

People who had no money accepted the little treat gratefully and hurried on by. But those who had a nickel to their name headed straight into Aunt Susan's store.

Aunt Milly saw us coming. "Well, it's my Bea!" she said, and I basked in the warmth of her smile. She always spoke of people that she loved as if they were her private property. It was wonderful belonging to Aunt Milly.

She looked so cute and girlish, with her bright auburn ringlets peeking out under the edges of her jaunty red toque, that no one would ever guess she was the mother of three children. And to hear her carefree laughter, no one would ever know that her husband was out of work too, just like Dad.

"What brings you downtown, Franny?" she asked, holding out the steaming scoop for me to help myself.

"Bea needs new shoes in the worst way," Mum said.

"Well, and who could deserve them more?" beamed my loving aunt.

"How have you been, Milly? You look kind of peaked."

"Why, I'm in the pink, Fran, just in the pink."

"Oh, pshaw, Milly," Mum clucked. "You always say that no matter what."

That's the way she was, Aunt Milly, always looking on the bright side.

"C'mon, Bea." She dug in her pocket and came up with a rusty old serving spoon. "You can help me dish out the samples while your mother visits Susan."

Oh, what fun it was! I felt like Lady Bountiful, spooning out the scrumptious cashew nuts and popping them into my mouth any time I liked. Then and there I decided to be a store lady when I grew up, just like Aunt Susan.

I could see Mum talking to her in the shop window. She kept right on working while she chatted, heaving a big batch of shiny redskins out of the boiling oil and resting the wire basket on a peg at the back of the cooker. She shook the basket once or twice and the golden oil streamed back into the black iron pot ready for the next batch. With her free hand she waved at me through the steamy window.

About ten minutes later Mum came scurrying out the open door with a box of hot nuts in one hand and our overdue transfers in the other. "Hurry, Bea," she called on the run, "or our transfers won't be worth a wooden nickel." I dropped the spoon clattering into the scoop and scampered after her to the streetcar stop at the corner.

"Love you!" Aunt Milly called after us. She was one of those rare people who could holler that right out loud and not care who heard it. I threw her back a kiss.

According to the time punched on our transfers we were fifteen minutes late, and stopovers were strictly forbidden by the Toronto Transit Commission.

My Uncle William worked for the T.T.C. Sometimes he was the conductor on the Yonge Street line and if we were lucky enough to get on his car we didn't have a thing to worry about. But if the conductor was a stranger we could be in trouble. Once we got caught red-handed with late transfers and got put right off the streetcar in disgrace. But this time we boarded with a crowd and the conductor was too busy to notice so we got away scot-free.

We settled ourselves on the circular seat at the back and Mum handed me the box of nuts. All the way down Yonge Street we munched and chattered and gazed out the mud-streaked windows. And whenever the streetcar jerked to a stop I went for a free slide around the shiny crescent seat.

Yonge Street hummed and sparkled in the early spring sunshine. Cars honked and horses whinnied. Dogs barked, bicycle bells jangled and the popcorn man's whistle blew a long thin note.

I read all the signboards as we passed. "Smoke Sweet Caporal," "Buy British Consul" and "Drink Coca-Cola." Boy, how I'd love to drink Coca-Cola. I had no idea what it tasted like, but the beautiful girl on the billboard said, "It's delicious!"

"I love Yonge Street, don't you, Mum?"

"Yes," she said, chewing a Brazil nut with her front teeth because the back ones had been bothering her lately. "And did you know, Bea, that it's the longest street in the world?"

"I didn't know that, Mum!"

"Well, you learn something every day."

Helen Hayes and Clark Gable were in a talkie at Loew's Theatre. I hadn't seen a talking picture yet, but Mum said when she had enough money she'd take me.

"Ka-ween Street!" bellowed the conductor. "Eaton's! Simpson's! Have your fares ready. This way out!" He pulled a lever by the fare box and the double doors clunked open. We jostled our way to the sidewalk.

Woolworth's Five-And-Ten-Cent Store stood on the corner of Queen and Yonge. And huddled in the swinging doorway was Old Blind Bill (that's what the sign said that hung around his neck).

"I'm sorry, Bill," Mum murmured as we passed.

"I didn't know you knew Blind Bill, Mum," I said.

"Shush, Bea," she said. "I only know him to see."

Toronto's two biggest department stores faced each other across Queen Street: the T. Eaton Company on the north and the Robert Simpson Company on the south. A steady stream of shoppers dodged each other to get to the opposite side. But Mum and I never went to Simpson's because Mum was a dyed-in-the-wool Eatonian.

We squeezed into the revolving doors together and let ourselves be swept inside. Then we stopped at the foot of Timothy Eaton's statue to wait for Aunt Hester, Uncle William's wife.

It was sort of a custom to meet at the store-founder's monument. And while you waited you gave his big bronze toe a rub for good luck. Mum said that was silly superstition, but she gave the shiny spot a quick little pat just in case.

"I remember the day he was buried," she mused, looking up into the bearded bronze face. "I was just a little bit of a thing and Puppa put me up on his shoulders so I could see. I can still feel the hush that fell over the crowd as the hearse went by. And following it came hundreds of carriages, all draped in black."

I loved to hear stories of the olden days. But before Mum had a chance to say any more we saw Aunt Hester bouncing towards us between the counters, her curls bobbing like little gold springs around her face.

Mum was a bit jealous of Aunt Hester. "She's got neither chick nor child and more money than she knows what to do with," she sighed enviously.

I knew this was true because I heard Mum tell Dad once that Uncle William brought home sixteen dollars every single week.

"Hello there, Tinker!" cried Aunt Hester breathlessly. She always called me Tinker.

The two of them had a little chat, then we made our way down the stairs and through the underground tunnel to the Annex. The tunnel ran under Albert Street. It always smelled of paint and turpentine. It was kind of a nice smell.

We stopped to watch a man demonstrate some cleaning fluid. First he smeared black grease on a patch of carpet. Then he removed it, clean as a whistle, with his magic cleaner. Aunt Hester got carried away and bought a large bottle for fifty cents.

The Annex was Eaton's bargain store. Its basement was a dank, smelly place with low-hanging pipes and uneven, littered wood floors. Mum hated the Annex. She said if Dad ever got working steady again it wouldn't see her for dust.

The basement was crowded, as usual, with crabby, frazzled mothers and whiny, dirty-nosed kids. Mountains of dry goods were piled up on big square tables. Mum stopped at every table to pick things over. Aunt Hester bought Uncle William a set of long drawers for ninety-nine cents and two pairs of socks for a quarter.

"If I had your money, Hester," Mum said, watching her sister-in-law peel off a two-dollar bill from a fat wad, "I wouldn't come near this place. I'd stick to the Main Store where everything is first class. Just look at this stuff, all soiled and messy." She flicked at the second-class goods disdainfully.

"There's not a thing wrong with these socks," replied Aunt Hester indignantly. "And my Thor will take out the spots in these drawers in the very first wash."

Mum winced at the mention of the Thor. I thought how dumb it was that Aunt Hester, with neither chick nor child, should own a washing machine while Mum, with all us kids, had to scrub on the washboard.

Mum was holding up a corselet, eyeing it critically. The flesh-coloured garment had two huge scoops in the front. I looked down at my flat chest and couldn't even imagine ever fitting into such a thing.

By this time my legs were killing me, so I hung onto the table edge and let them go all limp. It felt good. At last they got sick of underwear and we headed for the shoe department.

The minute I laid eyes on them I knew I had to have them. They were black patent leather with white patent bows and they were absolutely gorgeous. I could see myself in Sunday School swinging my feet out for Mr. Henderson, the Superintendent, to see.

Mum was paying a lot of attention to a pair of sturdy brown oxfords, so I grabbed the patents and shoved them under her nose.

"Please, Mum, can I have these?" I begged. "I promise I won't run in them, and I'll take them off after four every day."

"Oh, pshaw, Bea." She was smiling so I knew I had a chance. "You're too much of a scatterbrain to remember not to run. You'd have those flimsy slippers scuffed out in no time."

"No, Mum, I wouldn't! I'm not a scatterbrain!" For the first time I really resented the silly nickname. "I won't run—honest—I'll walk slow and careful all the time."

"Perhaps the young lady would like to try them on," came a man's silky voice from behind. The shoe salesman looked for all the world like the picture of Warner Baxter stuck up on our bedroom wall.

Mum didn't speak quickly enough, and before she knew it, he was down on his knees slipping them on my feet.

In spite of my brown ribbed stockings wrinkling around my ankles, the shoes looked beautiful. I got up and began to strut to show them off. I guess I looked unusually pleased with myself because Mum gave in sooner than I dared to hope.

"How much are they?" she asked Warner Baxter.

"They're a terrific buy at fifty cents," he assured her. "Only last week they were selling for ninety-nine cents and going like hotcakes. This is my last pair, an Opportunity Day special."

"Are you sure they fit, Bea?" Mum said. "They're final clearance so we can't bring them back, you know."

"I'm sure, Mum," I said.

"All right then." She couldn't resist a genuine bargain. And the price tickled her pink. Seeing she was in such a good mood, I begged to wear them home. She said that I could if I

# MOTHERS! YOU SHOULD BUY
## You'll Find These Values Outstanding

### Black Patent

**662-633.** Black Patent Boudoir Slippers. They have padded soles, low wood heels and dainty poms. Sizes 11, 12, 13, 1, 2 (no half sizes).
Per pair..... **79c**

### Sport Oxfords

Sturdy Suntan and Brown Leather Sport Oxfords with husky "No Trax" soles and heels. Just the thing for run-about wear because they'll stand lots of hard usage. No half sizes.
**662-636.** Misses' sizes 11, 12, 13, 1, 2. Per pair...... **1.35**
**662-637.** Child's sizes 6, 7, 8, 9, 10. Per pair........ **1.10**

### Snappy Oxfords

**662-582.** Just the thing for the modern miss with a flair for style. These Gunmetal Leather Oxfords with the new strap and buckle sport effect are bound to be popular. Have low heels with rubber top lifts. Sizes 11 to 2 (including half sizes).

**1** **98**
**Pair**

### Blue Felt

Pretty little Blue Felt Ribbon-Drawn Slippers, with Fawn-colored vamps and padded soles and heels. So cosy! No half sizes.
**662-655.** Misses' sizes 11, 12, 13, 1, 2. Pair..... **53c**
**662-656.** Child's sizes 8, 9, 10. Pair........... **49c**

### "Jingle Bells"

**662-673.** Sure to please the kiddies, these Blue Felt padded-sole Slippers with Red tops and jingling bells. A decided novelty. Sizes 5, 6, 7, 8, 9, 10. Per pair.. **69c**

### The "Cavalier"

**662-632.** Child's Blue Felt "Cavalier" model Slippers, with Red collars and neat pompoms; padded soles. Sizes 5, 6, 7, 8, 9, 10 only. Per pair..... **65c**

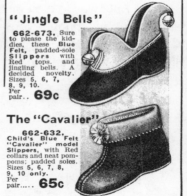

promised not to scuff them. Warner Baxter wrapped up my old shoes and handed me the package.

From the shoe department we went straight to the Annex lunch counter. It was a stand-up counter with no stools. Aunt Hester treated herself and Mum to a red-hot and a Vernor's and they both shared them with me. First I had a bite of Mum's red-hot, then a bite of Aunt Hester's. I watched a bit worriedly as the level of the sparkling drink crept lower in their glasses. They were chatting and sipping and seeming to pay no attention to me. But they both remembered to save me the last long slurp at the end.

After that we went to the Main Store, just looking. Instead of the elevators, we rode the moving stairs because Mum knew I liked them best. I always got an excited, scary feeling as we curved over the top and the moving stairs disappeared beneath our feet. Arthur told me once about a boy who got sucked in by his shoelaces and ended up a pile of mincemeat. But that couldn't happen to me today because my new shoes were slip-ons.

By the time we were on our way home, my feet were killing me. I knew five minutes after I put them on that my beautiful patent-leather slippers were at least two sizes too small.

"How do your new shoes feel, Bea?" Mum asked as we stepped off the streetcar. She must have read my mind!

"Just fine, Mum." My face turned beet-red with the big fat lie, but she didn't seem to notice.

# 14

# A fair exchange

Willa had the supper on when we got home. Mum had left a note pinned to the kitchen curtain telling her what to do, but Willa didn't really need instructions. Quite often she just ignored the note and did what she liked. Mum didn't mind. She loved surprises.

Dad came in behind us, with Billy on his arm and Jakey trailing after. Arthur wasn't home yet because he had a job with Andy, the baker, after school and on Saturdays. Mum said he could keep the job as long as he didn't fall behind in his school work. She always put education first. She said some people, especially those from the old countries, were more interested in the "almighty dollar" than in their children's futures. "Shove them out to work and rake in the money. That's all they care about!" she said disdainfully. I hoped and prayed Arthur wouldn't fall behind in his school work, because sometimes Andy gave him stale doughnuts as well as his twenty-five cents a week"

"How do you like Bea's new shoes?" Mum asked Willa.

"They're nice," Willa said.

Then I had to prance around and show them off to Dad while Mum went on about what a bargain they were.

At last I escaped to the bathroom. Off came my beautiful patents, and my swollen feet almost yelled out loud. I washed them in cold water even though they didn't need it because Mum had made me take a bath before we went downtown. The pain eased off a little. I dried them gingerly, then slipped into my soft old bedroom slippers and tried not to hobble down the stairs.

Mum noticed instantly. "Where are your new shoes, Bea?"

"I'm trying to keep them nice," I answered piously.

"That's a good girl," she said, obviously pleased.

The rest of the week I suffered the tortures of the damned. True to my promise, I didn't run or scuff. In fact I could hardly walk at all. Back and forth to school I went with tiny, painful steps, just like the poor little Chinese girls with bound-up feet that the missionaries were always telling us about in Sunday School.

On Friday I limped home and crawled up the stairs on all fours. Luckily, Mum was in the cellar. Tears running down my cheeks, I lowered my raw, blistered, swollen feet into the blessed cold water of the bathtub.

But I forgot to lock the door. And there stood Mum.

"For mercy sakes, what's wrong with your feet?" She dropped the clean towels and grabbed my feet in both hands. "Bea!" her voice rose in anger. "Did your new shoes do this?"

Sobbing with pain and shame, I blubbered out the truth.

Both Mum and Dad were mad as hornets. Dad ranted and raved about all the things fifty cents would buy. Mum even listed them: twenty pounds of cane sugar; ten loaves of stale bread; four pounds of creamery butter; oceans of milk and miles of toilet paper.

Willa and Arthur jumped on the bandwagon. "I needed new shoes worse than you!" snapped my long-suffering sister. And she did, too. Only that morning I had seen her cutting out another pair of corrugated insoles.

"Stupid, selfish pig!" hissed Arthur. His boots needed half-soling too.

"You deserve a good thrashing," Dad threatened balefully, and I shuddered at the thought of the strop on the bathroom door.

Tears rolling down my face, I edged my way out of the kitchen. Jakey's big, reproachful eyes followed me from under the table. Even Billy howled at me. I guess he was just holler-ing from hunger or colic or both, but I felt so guilty I took it personally.

The next day, Saturday, Mum marched me straight back to Eaton's. She was mad all the way and didn't speak once. I hated that worse than a licking. We took the short route and didn't go near Aunt Susan's.

We found Warner Baxter in the shoe department and Mum told him the whole awful story. Dangling my patents at arm's length, his moustache curled up in a sneer, he said coldly, "I'll have to speak to the manager. There's no exchange on 'clear-ance' you know," and walked away in a huff.

Two red spots appeared on Mum's cheeks. She rubbed her hands together in that nervous way she had and began pacing in circles on her dainty high heels. (She always managed to get beautiful sample shoes for next to nothing because her feet were so tiny.) I couldn't help but notice how pretty she looked with her cheeks all rosy and her eyes flashing like lights on water.

Warner Baxter came back with Rudolph Valentino, of all people! At least that's who the manager looked like to me. He had the same dark eyes and black patent leather hair.

"May I be of service, Miss?"

*Miss!* Could he mean Mum, the mother of all us kids?

She told the sad tale again in a voice that would melt an iceberg.

"Now, don't you worry your pretty little head." He gave Mum's arm a little squeeze and the red spots on her cheeks grew brighter. "You just leave everything to me." Looking Mum up and down from her dark wavy head to her small dainty feet, he whisked away my shoes.

The mad expression had left her face and she seemed to be holding back a smile.

"I think he likes you, Mum," I ventured.

"Shush, Booky," she said. I knew she wasn't mad any more.

Warner Baxter went by balancing a pyramid of shoe boxes and shot me a withering look. It was all I could do to stop my tongue from sticking out.

Then Rudolph came back carrying a sturdy pair of brown oxfords. "Now, let's see if these fit the young lady," he said, sitting me down and lacing the oxfords on to my injured feet. Oh, how good they felt! Roomy at the toe and absolutely perfect at the heel.

"Up you get and show them off to your charming mother," said oily old Rudolph. Then he added to Mum, "I can scarcely believe you're the mother of this big girl."

"How do they feel, Bea?" asked Mum, ignoring him as best she could.

"Terrific!" It was the latest word in school. Everything was terrific. "Really terrific!"

"Then we'll call it a fair exchange," said Rudolph, leering openly at Mum now. "And if I may be of any further service, you may come to me directly."

Nudging me nervously ahead of her, Mum hurried out of the basement.

"Wasn't he a nice man, Mum?" I chirped happily in my new shoes, knowing she wasn't mad any more. "Let's buy all our shoes from him, Mum, so we won't have to worry if they fit or not. Do you think he looked like Rudolph Valentino, or more like Ramon Navarro?" Ramon Navarro was the latest movie hero Willa had stuck up on our bedroom wall.

"He couldn't hold a candle to either one of them," she answered huffily. "And he's got shifty eyes and B.O. and I don't want to hear another word about it. Now, let's go and have ourselves a treat."

At the far end of the tunnel we stopped in front of a refreshment stand. Mum bought a five-cent paper cupful of "The Drink You Eat With A Spoon" and she asked for two wooden spoons so we could share it. It was a delicious chocolatey-malty concoction, as smooth and cool as ice cream.

After that we did the most amazing thing. We went to Shea's Hippodrome on Bay Street across from the City Hall. There we saw John Boles on the stage singing, "K–K–K–Katie!" and a young red-headed comedian named Red Skelton who put on the funniest act I had ever seen. He pantomimed a lady getting dressed in the morning, wiggling into an imaginary girdle and struggling to hook up a brassiere behind his back. Without uttering a word he had the whole theatre in stitches.

It was a wonderful show and I clapped until my hands hurt. But what followed was more wonderful by far. I saw my first talking picture. It was called "Pack Up Your Troubles," starring Stan Laurel and Oliver Hardy. It was so funny I nearly wet my bloomers. I had seen Laurel and Hardy once before in a silent picture, but oh, they were a million times funnier in the talkies. I became a movie fan for life.

I couldn't get over the talkies. Twice Willa had taken me to the Kingswood in Birchcliff to see silents. But they didn't compare to the talkies. What joy it was just to sit there and listen and not have to read the lines. I could never read them fast enough and Willa said I spoiled the whole show by begging her to read out loud.

On our way home that day everything went right. The sun was shining, my feet were purring, and we got on Uncle William's streetcar. We sat opposite him on the wooden slat seat and he smiled and winked at me. I glanced around to see if anybody had noticed. I was awfully proud of him sitting up there importantly in the conductor's box.

"How are you and Jim getting along, Franny?" he asked between stops.

"Oh, I can't complain, William."

She was in a good mood!

When we got up to leave Uncle William put his hand over the glass fare box to let Mum know she didn't have to pay. Then he gave us each a transfer, and since we walked from the city limits, we got all the way home for free.

Strolling up Kingston Road in the balmy spring air, we talked a blue streak. I asked Mum a million questions about the movie and she answered every one. That's the way she was, my mum. She never held a grudge.

# 15

# My dad, the hero

The first Sunday in May was as warm as summer. We were still living in the new house. Mr. Ratman had been by a few times but he hadn't put us out yet. He just gave Dad fair warning that the rent was overdue.

Mum was doing a lot of nagging lately, and Dad had gone all quiet, like the air before a storm. And then he had a stroke of luck. He got two weeks work painting fences. It was the first wage he had earned in a dog's age, but not the first work he had done. He had put in lots of back-breaking hours doing pogey jobs to earn our relief voucher, hard jobs like breaking up sidewalks and shovelling snow off roofs and cleaning streets and sewers. He always felt better about taking the relief voucher when he had worked for it.

When he got paid for painting the fences he gave Willa and Arthur and me two big copper pennies. We liked the big coins best because they looked like more than the little one-cent pieces.

We knew, without being told, that one was for Sunday School and one was for anything we liked. I could hardly wait to drop mine in the collection plate. I hoped Mr. Henderson would notice the noise it made as much as he noticed the silence that fell when my hand was empty.

I really enjoyed Sunday School that day. We sang some nice hymns. My favourite was "Black and yellow, red and white, they are precious in his sight . . ."

Sometimes I wished I had a black or yellow or red friend. I didn't know anybody from another country. I had seldom even seen a person of a different colour. But I met a Catholic girl once. Her name was Ursula. She went to a strange school called "Separate." Only she was white just like me.

After the hymn singing Mrs. Wardell acted out the story where Jesus tells his disciples to let the children come unto him and forbid them not. She played the part of Jesus and all us kids were the children. Then we finished with the prayer Jesus made up himself, the one that started out "Our father, witchart in heaven, hollow be thy name" and ended up "forever and ever alllmen."

When we got home we changed into our old clothes and Dad suggested we go for a walk while Billy was sleeping so Mum could make the supper in peace. So off we went up Warden Avenue towards Prob's Bush. Jakey rode on Dad's shoulders and Willa walked beside them. Arthur and I ran on ahead.

The sun was as warm as toast so we took off our Star Box sweaters that Mum had made us wear so we wouldn't catch a spring cold. Arthur tied his around his neck by the arms, and I followed suit.

Arthur hated that sweater. He wore it twice to school and then flatly refused to put it on again. When Mum asked why, he explained that the kids who didn't have one (those whose fathers were working and didn't get a Star Box) made fun of the kids who did. They hollered "Tiger! Tiger!" at us because of the orange and black stripes. Even Arthur's best friend, Lloyd Armstrong, poked fun at the sweater. When Lloyd saw it on Christmas Day, he was green with envy. But when he found out it was a charity sweater he joined in jeering with the rest.

Being called "Tiger" didn't bother me much because there were more of us tigers than anybody else in the schoolyard. But when I overheard Old-Lady-Rice-Pudding refer to our sweaters as the "uniform of the poor," it really made me squirm.

We were nearly to the railroad underpass when we heard the train coming. Breaking into a run, we called over our shoulders for Willa to hurry up. Putting her dignity aside, she ran like the wind to catch us. We made it just in time, as the Canadian Pacific thundered overhead. We closed our eyes and made our secret wishes. You had to finish wishing before the last boxcar trundled over or it didn't have a chance of coming true.

"I wish I pass into Senior Third in June," I said out loud, since nobody could hear me. Then I added, "In Jesus name, alllmen!" for good measure—and because it was Sunday. And because I needed all the help I could get. The barbed-wire fence surrounding Prob's Bush had the same scary sign hanging on it that had been there last year. *Private Property! Keep Out! Trespassers Will Be Prosecuted!*

Then Dad did the same brave thing he'd done before. Without batting an eye he lifted Jakey over the forbidden fence, jumped over it himself, and held it down with his foot for Willa and Arthur and me to step across. I couldn't get over how fearless he was.

"Doesn't Dad know that trespassers will be executed?" I whispered to Willa.

"Not executed, silly, prosecuted," she explained.

I didn't know what the difference was, so I decided to ask Arthur. "What's prosecuted, Arthur?"

"Prosecuted means executed. It's the same thing, stupid!"

He sounded very sure of himself and I couldn't help but wonder if Willa was wrong for once. Anyway, I was sure proud of my dad because if Arthur was right and we got caught I knew it would be Dad who got hung by the neck until he was dead, and not us kids. Imagine being that brave, just to take your children for a nice spring walk.

The bush was budding out but it wasn't leafy yet. Thousands of pussy willows climbed up slender brown stalks. "Listen said the pussy willow, I can hear a brook. Spring is coming, spring is coming. Let's go out and look." I sang the words softly.

A fat brown cow was drinking from the creek. At the sight of her Jakey let out an excited squeal and she went crashing into the underbrush.

Dad stretched out on a grassy knoll and rested his head on a smooth rock. I folded my Star Box sweater and offered it to him for a pillow. "Thank you, Bea," he said, tucking it under his head and closing his eyes.

His wispy hair looked like spun gold in the sunlight. His pale skin was stretched tightly over his raw-boned face. "He looks hungry," I thought. And he likely was. He ate little at mealtimes, always helping himself last. If there was meat, he ate the fat and gristle. If there weren't enough vegetables to go around, he did without. He drank his tea black, wetted his cereal with water and always took the heel of the bread. It was his way of doing his best for his family.

Arthur had step-stoned out to the middle of the creek. He had one of Mum's quart jars half full of pollywogs already. Jakey was darting every which way after snakes and frogs and butterflies. I was uneasy that he might fall into the deep end of the creek, but a glance at Dad relieved my mind. His eyes were only half closed.

Willa and I wandered off into the bush for wildflowers. Mum liked it when we brought her home a nosegay for the table. In no time at all I had a fistful of violets. I was just about to pick some white lilies, growing thick about my feet, when Willa stopped me.

"Don't pick those!" she cried. "It's against the law." Quickly I drew back my hand, not wanting to risk any more executions. "Trilliums are Ontario's provincial flower and if you pick them it kills the plant. That's why they are protected by law," Willa explained.

"How about these?" I asked, pointing to a patch of pink.

"It's okay to pick those. They're hepaticas. Oh, and here's some adder's-tongue. Mum likes these."

When we had a nice variety we headed back to the clearing. Dad was sitting up, his head tilted back, one hand shading his eyes from the westerly sun.

"Look there." He pointed with a scarred finger to the top of a tall pine tree. Perched on the tip, singing its heart out, was a brilliant bluebird. The sky paled behind it. Just then another, lighter bluebird joined it on the tip. They trilled prettily for a moment, then flew away together.

"Into the wild blue yonder," Dad said.

I'd never heard him say anything poetic before. And there was a dreamy look in his eyes. "That big old pine tree puts me in mind of the one I felled in France," he said. "Only it was bigger still."

"Tell us, Dad, tell us!" begged Arthur. He loved war stories. Especially the one about the pine tree, because our Dad was the hero of it.

"Well," began Dad, picturing in his mind's eye that faraway forest in France, "it was the spring of '17, a terrible, wet, cold spring. It was raining cats and dogs that day and an old French farmer had come out to see what us 'Forresters' were up to. He pointed to the grey sky and kept repeating, *'Le guerre. . .le guerre.'* He was blaming the cannon's roar for the bad weather in his sunny homeland. We were so close to the front that day, we had to holler to be heard over the gunfire. But we didn't complain about the wet and cold and noise because we knew our comrades were wounded and dying up there."

Here he paused in his story, as he always did, to reverently remember his fallen comrades. We waited respectfully. "Me and me mates were on lumberjack duty making a road for the troops," he continued, "and the Sergeant Major had given me a direct order to fell a certain giant pine. He cut a notch in the bark to show me where to begin. Well now, being raised as I was in the bush in Muskoka, I knew that if I was to carry out his orders that giant pine would be bound to fall right across our front lines. I wasn't one to question authority, mind, but I realized that if I didn't speak up some of our brave boys would be killed, and not by enemy gunfire either. Begging his pardon at the top of my lungs, I predicted where the tree would fall. He scratched his head and looked mighty skeptical, so I took a stick and drew a picture on the wet ground. Finally he motioned me to carry on, so I swung my axe and made my wedge, on the opposite side to his, and began to chop. And that big French pine tree fell just as neat as you please, exactly where I said it would. The pine needles were still flying when the Sergeant Major clapped me on the back. He was a fine officer. I never served under any better."

"Tell us more stories, Dad," I pleaded. "Tell us about being on leave in London. Are there lions and tigers in Piccadilly Circus, Dad?"

"No, Bea," he laughed, "It's not that kind of circus. Piccadilly is the centre of London where the streets all come together like the hub of a wagon wheel."

"Tell us about when you and Uncle Charlie went to visit Beatrice Baillie in London, Dad," put in Willa unexpectedly.

Dad grinned at the memory. "Well, as you know, Bea Baillie is a famous comedian of stage and screen—and she's also Lady Bolton, since she married the old Lord. She's cousin to me on my faither's side (that's how Dad said "father") so Charlie and I decided to pay her a call. The first person we asked directed us to her house. Everybody in London knew where Bea Baillie lived. It was a big old mansion off Russell Square and the butler answered our knock. 'Tell Miss Baillie her cousins are here from Canada,' says Charlie, bold as brass. 'One moment, gentlemen,' says the butler suspiciously, and shuts the door in our face. Back he comes and opens the door a crack. 'Lady Bolton thinks she has no relatives in Canada,' says he. Well, that got Charlie's dander up so he hollers through the crack, 'You tell her to think again and maybe she'll remember picking blueberries with us on our father's farm in Muskoka.' Then I put in my two cents worth. 'Tell her ladyship for me, just to jog her memory, that her grandma and my grandma are the same grandma!' Then Charlie yells, 'And if that don't make us kissing cousins I'll eat my khaki shirt!'

"That did it. The door swung open and there she was, the funniest woman in the world. That's how she was billed at the London Palladium. 'Hello, Jim,' she says as nice as pie. 'How are you, Charlie? Sorry for keeping you waiting, but I can't be too careful. I'm in a dreadful hurry to get to the theatre. Would you like some passes to my show? Can I offer you a spot of tea?' We said no thanks to the tea and thank you very much to the passes. It was a wonderful show. We were mighty proud of Bea that night, even if her head was too big for her hat. That's where your name comes from, Bea."

I never knew that before! Imagine skinny little scatter-brained me being named after the funniest woman in the world. Right then and there I decided to be an actress when I grew up.

"Tell us more, Dad," begged Arthur. "Tell us about the time you nearly got your ear shot off."

Dad rubbed the jagged scar with blunt fingers. "Later maybe. Right now we've got to be making tracks. Your mother will have the supper ready."

"Wait a minute," Willa said. "I want to take a picture."

She had brought along her Brownie camera. She had got it free from the Kodak company for being born in 1918. Every Canadian baby born the year of the Armistice got a free Brownie. The only trouble was, Willa could hardly ever afford a film. But she had some that day because Uncle Charlie had given her a shinplaster for her birthday and she'd gone right out and bought a film.

She told us to sit close together on the grass and keep perfectly still. *Click!* went the Brownie, and that lovely, springy day was captured forever on celluloid.

We could hear Mum singing through the open door as we came up the walk. "Mother, may I go out to swim? Yes, my darling daughter. Hang your clothes on the hickory limb, and don't go near the water."

The new house was awash with delicious smells. We were all just about starving and for once there was enough for everybody: golden meatloaf swimming in caramel-coloured gravy, clouds of mashed potatoes overflowing the mixing bowl and green peas peeking in and out of bright orange carrot rings.

The nosegay looked pretty on the white, threadbare tablecloth. Mum said it was prettier than roses.

"There's dessert," Mum said when the last crumb was gone. She went to the back porch and brought in a covered bowl. She lifted the lid and out came the beautiful aroma of oranges and bananas all sliced up together.

When I grew up, that tangy blend of flavours always brought saliva rushing to my mouth and memories rushing to my mind of that sweet spring day in 1933.

# 16
# Dead-end Veeny Street

We had to leave the new house after only five months. Mr. Ratman caught us at the supper table when Mum had the kitchen door open airing out the house. His eyes were sad as he handed Dad the eviction notice, and there was a drip on the end of his nose. He sniffed and made it disappear. I didn't hate him any more.

The house-hunting started again, and so did the fighting. Mum was mad and upset about leaving the new house. She loved its hardwood floors and dry cement cellar and the breezy balcony that we had only just begun to use.

Sometimes Mum had fits of rage that changed suddenly into wild, hysterical laughter. Then the laughter would give way unexpectedly to wretched, heart-rending sobs. It was awful, seeing her like that.

Dad was just the opposite, cold and silent and sullen, his thin face turning grey as ashes. He wasn't the same Dad at all that had risked his neck to take us kids to the forbidden bush for a nice spring walk.

Once again they came home with fistfuls of latchkeys. And once again they fought over where we would move to. As before, there was no shortage of houses. *For Rent* signs sprouted like toadstools all over the city of Toronto. People were always on the move in an effort to keep one jump ahead of the bailiff. Sometimes families were actually put out on the street. You'd see them standing forlornly on the sidewalk amid their furniture. "Like lost souls," Mum would sigh, "with no place to go."

The day before this was about to happen to us, Mum came home with red patches tingeing her high cheekbones and a skeleton key in her hand.

"It's the key to Billy and Maude Sundy's house in Swansea," she announced breathlessly. "Puppa persuaded them to let me have it. He told them we'd make good tenants, Jim. He said you were a willing handyman and I was a spotless house-keeper."

"How much rent do they want?" was all Dad said.

"Eight dollars a month." Mum's voice held a defiant ring.

"That's a lot of money."

"Billy and Maude are good Christians and they're Puppa's friends. They won't put us out."

"Is Billy and Maude's house near Grampa's, Mum?" I asked hopefully.

"Just a hop, skip and jump through the lane, Booky."

Since we were due to be thrown out the very next day, there was no time for argument. So it was settled.

Uncle Charlie moved us in his beat-up old truck. There wasn't room for everybody in the cab, and Mum wouldn't hear of Wins and Arthur and me riding in the back with the furniture, so we had to take the streetcar to Swansea.

The streetcar we got on had reversible wicker seats. Arthur

110

took hold of the metal handgrip and flipped the backrest over so we could ride facing each other. Then I got sick from going backwards. Willa got up and asked the conductor for transfers so we could get off and get some fresh air. But he just ignored her and kept us standing on the door treadle stop after stop, with me barely holding back the sick. At last a grown-up wanted off so he had to ring the driver to stop. Then Willa had to beg for transfers because we didn't have any more carfare. It mortified her to beg like that, but she knew I couldn't help being sick so she didn't get mad.

All three of us kids were sorry to leave Birchcliff. Between the old house and the new house we had lived there a record two and a half years. We were all leaving friends behind. By the time we got to Swansea, I was already pining away for Audrey.

Billy and Maude's house wasn't much to write home about. It was one of four tall skinny stuck-together houses on dead-end Veeny Street. White scrolly woodwork decorated the four peaked roofs. Inside, narrow rooms were piled, like shoe-boxes, one on top of the other. The cellar was just a hole dug in the soft sand underneath the kitchen. Narrow slat stairs, like a homemade ladder, led down into its earthy depths.

"It'll be a good place to store vegetables," Mum said.

There was no furnace in the dugout, so our coal stove would have to heat the kitchen and the tiny bedroom above it. There was a Quebec heater in the dining room with a pipe going through the middle bedroom on its way to the roof.

"That'll give the girls a nice warm pipe to dress by in wintertime," Mum said.

The boys' bedroom at the front of the house had no heat at all.

The kitchen was painted an ugly grey from the cracked linoleum floor to the tin-tiled ceiling.

"We'll change it to cream and green," Mum said.

"Where'll the money come from?" grumbled Dad.

Mum ignored him. "At least the house is clean."

The tiny, cramped front room was joined to the narrow dining room by a scrolly wooden archway. Both rooms were covered from their foot-high baseboards to their ten-foot ceilings in peeling, brown-stained paper.

"We'll get some nice flowered paper from Eaton's," Mum said. "They sell off bundle lots for next to nothing in the tunnel."

I'd never seen my mother so cheerful about a move before. I guess that's because she was back home in Swansea where she was born and raised. Her grandparents, all four them, had been among the first settlers in the little village. They'd named it after Swansea in Wales.

The minute Arthur and Willa and I arrived that day I ran lickety-split in the front and out the back and through the lane to Grampa's.

"I'm here, Grampa!" I called in his back kitchen door.

He poked his wiry head around from the dining room. "Hello there, Be-*a*-trice. How's my girl?" he said.

Oh, how I loved being his girl. It made me feel special and important, like being a boy, or being adopted, or being the only girl in a family of boys. Ruthie Armstrong, who lived next door to the new house, was the youngest of seven children, all boys but her, and her father called her his little miracle.

Joey was sitting on a three-legged stool in the corner by the cold stove eating dried beans out of a honey pail. He kept giving me the evil eye. I knew he wasn't glad to see me, and I think he was jealous of me too. When I told this to Mum she said, "Poor little gaffer. He's stuck like glue to Puppa since Mumma went 'home.' "

Grampa sat down by the table and lit his sawed-off corncob. He tamped it down with a tobacco stained thumb and drew in the flame from a thick wooden match while I told him all about our trip out on the streetcar. He had on a grey flannel undershirt with fireman's braces on top and I noticed how stooped his shoulders were. Mum said that was from shovelling coal into the blast furnace at the Bolt Works for forty-odd years. The Bolt Works was a terrible sweatshop in those days, she said. Six days a week and ten hours a day with never a holiday.

But Grampa was luckier than most, she said—at least he still had all his fingers and thumbs. Not like poor old Andy McCrae who lost half his hand in a Bolt Works accident and then was forever thankful because they didn't fire him. After all, he reasoned, who'd want to hire a cripple with only one good hand?

I didn't stay very long that first day. Joey made me nervous, cracking beans and giving me the evil eye, so I kissed Grampa under his overgrown, tea-stained moustache and promised to come back the very next day to trim it for him.

Flying back the way I'd come, through the lane, in the back door and out the front, I made a beeline across the road to Gladie's.

Gladie was my cousin once-removed. There were seven children in her family and when they saw me coming they all ran

out to meet me. Then some twice-removed cousins spilled out of the stuck-together houses, and Arthur came leaping down our front porch steps to join the pack. There must have been twenty of us kids, all laughing and joking and kicking up the dust in the middle of the road on unpaved, dead-end Veeny Street.

Buster, Gladie's big red-headed brother, pulled a nickel from his overall pocket and cried, "C'mon, gang, treats on me!"

So up the street we followed him, like the pied piper, to Hunter's corner grocery store.

Mr. Hunter was behind the counter weighing some white sugar in a brown paper bag. "Will there be anything else, Mrs. Medd?" he asked pleasantly while scrunching the sugar bag closed.

"I'll have six pieces of bologna, sliced thin, and add it to my bill please, Mr. Hunter," said Mrs. Medd, glaring at us noisy kids over her glasses.

The grocer ripped a square of shiny paper off a wide roll that was bolted to the counter top and placed it under the slicing machine. Pressing a long tube of pink bologna firmly against the circular blade, he turned the handle rhythmically. The meat, sliced thin as she said, piled up in the centre of the paper. Then he folded it into a neat, flat package. A ball of string was held prisoner in a wire cage behind the counter. The string ran up to the ceiling, through a series of wire loops, and dangled down over the grocer's bald head. Reaching up without looking, he grabbed it, tied the parcel, snapped the string and let it go. It retracted towards the ceiling automatically.

The bell jangled over the door as Mrs. Medd left the store.

116

Now Mr. Hunter patted his aproned potbelly, scratched his shiny bare head and winked at Arthur and me.

"I see you folks got here," he said. "Remember me to your mother. Now, what can I do you for?" He chuckled at his own joke.

"I want five cents worth of penny candy, Mr. Hunter," said Buster, importantly showing his nickel.

"Well, help yourself, Buster," said Mr. Hunter. Then he handed me the heel of the bologna.

I was just about to hide it in my pinny-pocket when Arthur said, "Bits on you!" and grabbed my hand and took a great big bite. Darn that Arthur!

Buster went behind the counter and studied the candy display in the store window. There was a wonderful assortment: blackballs with caraway-seed centres, licorice pipes, sherbets, chocolate brooms, miniature ice cream cones stuffed with stale marshmallow, and little round discs with messages written in red dye: *Be Mine, Kiss Me, Ouch!, Hi Toots!* and stuff like that.

The grab bags were piled in the corner. They cost one cent each and if you were lucky there might be three cents worth of stale candy inside. Buster bought five grab bags and dumped them all out on the cement stoop. The he divvied it up. I got a pink disc that said *Good Luck*, which seemed like a good omen to me.

That night Mum said she was too busy to cook supper and we could help ourselves. So I made myself a bologna sandwich on the counter of the kitchen cabinet. Then I had a cup of water and a white-sugar sandwich. I was still hungry when I went to bed.

Dad had all the beds set up. Billy's cot was in the boys' room because Mum and Dad's room was barely big enough to hold their brown metal bed and bureau. The reason their room was so small was because the end had been chopped off to make a bathroom. It was the smallest bathroom I'd ever seen. The sink and bathtub were just about right for a midget family. Only the toilet was the regular size.

Our dresser wasn't set up yet, so Willa wouldn't be able to give me heck for throwing my clothes in the corner. The wooden floors were rough with chipped grey paint. I had a momentary twinge of regret, remembering the shiny golden hardwood of the new house.

I was just drifting off to sleep when I thought of something that woke me with a yelp. Catapulting out of the middle of our sagging mattress, I raced down the strange dark staircase.

Mum and Dad were still working. The flour bin was tilted on its hinges out of the kitchen cabinet and Mum was filling it from a Monarch bag. Dad was wiring a broken chair rung.

"Dad! Dad!" I bounded like a frightened deer through the cluttered dining room. They looked up in alarm, their faces drawn and tired.

"Good gracious! What's the matter?" cried Mum.

"My hoop and stick! I left it under the porch of the new house. Can we go back and get it in the morning, Dad? Before somebody steals it?"

"Don't be foolish," snapped Dad. "It's too far a piece to go for a homemade hoop and stick."

My face dropped a mile and I burst out crying.

"Don't cry, Bea." Dad's voice was suddenly gentle. "I'll make you a new one."

"Tomorrow, Dad? First thing? Promise?"

"Oh, all right. Now stop blubbering and get to bed."

He was as good as his word, my dad. Right after breakfast the next day he went out and found an old sulky wheel and a wooden slat. He did his best, I know, but the wheel wobbled and the crossbar was too short to steer it by. Try as I might I couldn't keep it up for more than half a block. So I put it away under the clothesline stoop, and never again did I have a hoop and stick to match the one that got left behind at the new house.

# 17

# A free ride on the Bug

Swansea was the best place in the world to live in summertime. Not only did we have all of Lake Ontario for our swimming hole, but Sunnyside Amusement Park was just a hop, skip and jump along the boardwalk. Twice that summer Willa took me there. The first time was best because it didn't rain.

Right after supper (Mum told us to run along, she'd do the dishes) we headed through the bush, up and down the hills and valleys of the "Camel's Back," and out onto opulent Ellis Avenue.

It was a hot, humid July night, as all July nights seemed to be in those days, and our dresses stuck to our legs as we walked.

"Whew," said Willa, mopping her brow, "I wish the free streetcars were still running."

"Free streetcars? Down Ellis Avenue?"

"No, silly, on Bloor Street. When I was your age the T.T.C. ran free streetcars along Bloor and down Roncesvalles. Then all Evie and I had to do was walk down the wooden steps into Sunnyside."

"Was it Depression then?"

"No. Dad had a steady job at Gutta Percha then."

"Well, why don't they run them now, when it's Depression and nobody's got any money?"

"I don't know. *C'est la vie*, I guess."

"What does 'say lah vee' mean?"

"It's French. It means that's life."

Boy, Willa was smart!

As we passed the dark, shiny waters of Grenadier Pond, I pictured the slimey green bones of the Grenadier Guards and their horses, all mingled together down there in the bottomless deep. Long years ago, in wintertime, the whole regiment had crashed through the ice and drowned. That's how the pond got its name. Or so the story goes. I sure felt sorry for those horses.

Under the railroad bridge we went, and across Lakeshore Road to the boardwalk.

The wide, weather-beaten boards rumbled pleasantly under the pounding of so many strolling feet. A cool breeze blew in off the lapping lake, ruffling our hair and soothing our sweaty brows.

Swansea's Point, the little peninsula we laid claim to, was almost deserted now. But a few intrepid bathers still romped in the blue-green water. And some girls in beach-pyjamas played catch on the soft white sand.

"There goes the Belly-Wart ice-wagon!" I cried, as the familiar horse-drawn van clip-clopped along Lakeshore, its backboard dribbling a steady stream of water.

"Not 'Belly-Wart,' dummy," sighed my long-suffering sister. "Bell-*U*-Art!"

Wafting on the wind from the Seabreeze Bandshell came the

sweet strains of "In the Good Old Summertime." Our hearts and running shoes hurried to the beat. I had to skippety-hop really fast to keep up with Willa.

"I see the roller coaster!" I squealed excitedly.

"Well naturally. It hasn't moved, you know." Sometimes the five years between us was hard for Willa to bear.

It looked like a giant Meccano toy etched against the deep blue sky. "The Flyer" was its name, and no wonder. The way it zipped around those hairpin turns and plummeted down those mountainous hills, it's a miracle it didn't take right off and go flying into space.

"The next time I get some money I'll take you on it," promised Willa. I think she was feeling bad about being sarcastic.

The minute we entered the concrete park my nose caught the tantalizing aroma of vinegar and chips. "I wish I had a nickel for a cone of chips," I moaned.

"You knew we didn't have any money when we left home," Willa reminded me sternly. So I put on my biggest pout and then she said, "Oh, never mind. We'll go and watch the water chute."

A rowboat had just emerged from the Tunnel of Love with a couple of spooners in it.

"What do they do in there, Willa?" I was pretty sure she'd know. She was fifteen.

"What makes you so dumb, Bea?"

I hated that. A question instead of an answer. And I couldn't even think of a smart reply.

We held our breath as the boat climbed the perpendicular hill and teetered, for a thrilling moment, at the brink of the rushing chute. Then the spooners screamed and I screamed as they plunged headlong into the sloshing water trough below. A giant wave flopped over the side, soaking our running shoes.

Oh, what I'd give to be terrified like that!

"C'mon, Bea, we haven't got all night," said Willa, stamping the water out of her sopping shoes.

We squished along, stopping for a minute to watch the cracking, whirling Whip and to stare up, wide-eyed, at the swooping Ferris wheel.

The Caterpillar stood idle, its green canvas skin folded back. I knew first-hand the thrill of being swallowed up in its billowing, wrinkly hide because my Aunt Hester had taken me on it once.

A fat weight-guesser in a sweaty undershirt eyed Willa up and down. He held out a gaudy doll with stuck-together legs and said in a wheedling voice, "Guess your weight, Miss? Only a nickel and I won't touch a thing."

"C'mon, Bea, we'll be late!" Blushing furiously, Willa yanked me by the arm.

"Ouch! Late for what?" I screeched.

"Oh, don't be so dopey!" she said, disgusted.

Well, at least it wasn't a question.

We passed the games of chance and stopped to watch the one we liked best. A man sat on a swing over a barrel of water. Then the player threw a baseball and if it hit the bull's-eye over the man's head he got dumped in the drink. We hung around until this happened (he came up gasping and snorting and yelling bad words) and then we continued on.

"I wish I had a nickel for the Fishpond," I lamented loudly.

You never knew when a rich stranger might be listening and take pity on you and hand you a nickel.

"You promised if I'd bring you, you wouldn't whine, Bea," Willa warned me with a frown.

What earthly good were all these wonders to a couple of Depression children without two cents to rub together? No good at all, unless they happened to have a relative who worked at Sunnyside. And we did! Our Auntie Gwen, Mum's third-to-the-youngest sister, was the ticket seller on the Custard Cars. Now the Custard Cars, cunning little automobiles that you drove all by yourself, were my very favourite ride in all the world.

"I hope Auntie Gwen is working tonight," I said anxiously.

"She is. I asked Mum," said my wonderful, practical sister.

And there she was, sitting in her little booth, looking a lot like Mum only younger. She was busy putting a roll of pink tickets on the spindle. When she was all set for business, she glanced up.

"Well, look who's here!" she said good-naturedly. "And how's every little thing?"

Willa said every little thing was fine. And we waited. Mum told us not to ask. Just wait and see, she said.

"Would you like a ride before we get too busy, Bea?"

"Yes please, Auntie Gwen!" I chirped, remembering my manners for a change.

Opening the little back door of the booth, she called out the magic words. "George, this is my niece. Give her a ride, will you?" Then she turned back to Willa. "You're too big for the Custard Cars, Willa, so you'll just have to be satisfied to chinwag with your auntie."

Poor Willa! Imagine having to be satisfied with a chinwag!

George told me to hop right into Number 22. Then he kicked something underneath and hollered, "Okay, girlie, step on the gas!"

I did, and away I went at breathtaking speed, alone on the open road. Oh, it was glorious! I could have spent the rest of my life in Car Number 22.

The "road" was a wide wooden track made in the shape of a figure eight. The top circle of the figure eight jutted out into a weedy, empty lot. It was so far away from Auntie Gwen's ticket booth, it was downright scary.

As I steered back to the starting point I pressed down hard on the gas and gave George a wide berth. But at the end of the second circuit, no amount of pressure would prevent Number 22 from coming to a stop.

"Didja run outta gas, girlie?" grinned George.

"Yep! Fill 'er up, George!" I answered cockily.

He laughed out loud and gave the underside of my car another magic kick and away I went again. Four times he gave my car a kick, and then the paying customers began to arrive.

"That's all for now, girlie," said George kindly, as he steered me over to the side.

I used my latest saying. "Thanks a bunch, George!"

"Hurry up, Bea!" Willa sounded impatient. I guess she was tired of all that chinwagging.

I remembered to thank Auntie Gwen, the way Mum said.

She looked at her watch and said, "It's early yet. Why don't you run down to the Bug and ask John for a ride?"

John was Auntie Gwen's new husband. He didn't know us from a hill of beans.

"He won't recognize us," said Willa doubtfully.

"Well, tell him who you are. Say I sent you."

It seemed too good to be true. We made a beeline through the thickening crowd.

Sure enough there he was, a tall, handsome, almost total stranger, standing high up on a wooden platform.

"That's him, Willa! That's him! Ask! Ask!"

"I'm not asking." Willa was shy about things like that. Mum said she was backward about coming forward.

So up the wooden steps I ran. "Are you John?"

"That's right." He looked puzzled.

"Auntie Gwen said to tell you who we are. I'm Bea and that's my sister Willa down there."

Willa was embarrassed to be pointed out, so she hung her head. John still looked puzzled, but before I had to explain any more his face lit up with a smile. (Boy, was he handsome when he smiled. I got my first big crush right then and there.)

"Oh, sure, you're Fran's children. Would you like a ride on the Bug before it gets busy?"

"Yes, please," I answered quickly.

"Okay, Willa," he called to her. "Up you come!"

The Bug was a grown-up ride, so Willa wasn't too big. Thank goodness, because in spite of the iron bar Uncle John snapped across our laps she had to hang on to me for dear life.

Round and round and up and down and over the twisty hills we flew, my sedate big sister screaming her head off just as loud as me. Three times our new uncle told us to "stay put" as he went about snapping people into the ladybug-shaped cars. When he finally unsnapped us we thanked him a bunch and staggered down the steps to solid ground.

We sat down on a green, wooden bench to get our land legs back. "We'd better be getting home," Willa said.

"Can we walk past the merry-go-round on our way?" I said.

She waited patiently as I gazed at the lovely prancing horses and thrilled to the loud music of the calliope. I picked out a horse that reminded me of Major, my grampa's horse in Muskoka. How I wished I could jump on his back and go galloping off in circles. But we had no money, and no more relatives who worked at Sunnyside.

"I'm starved," I said, sniffing the air as we neared a red-hot stand. "Let's look on the ground for money."

"Okay," Willa agreed. She seemed in a much better mood since our ride on the Bug. "But we won't find any."

She was right of course.

Tree-lined Ellis Avenue was very dark at night. Fireflies sparkled eerily all over the pitch-black pond. Bullfrogs croaked hoarsely in the rushes. Willa took my hand and we began to hurry. It was a long walk home.

Going in the back way through the yard, we could see Mum through the faded green mosquito netting on the kitchen window. She was sitting in the middle of the room under the dangling light bulb so she could see to mend a ladder in her stocking. The house was quiet with the little ones in bed.

"Did you girls have a good time?" She sounded tired.

"Uncle John gave us three free rides on the Bug," Willa burst out before I had a chance. "And is he ever handsome! And Bea had—oh, I don't know how many free rides on the Custard Cars."

"I wish I could go to Sunnyside every night all summer," I said. "Can we go back tomorrow night, Mum?"

"For mercy sakes, no," Mum said, clucking her tongue. "That would be too much of a good thing."

I already knew that, but there was no harm in asking.

"I'm hungry," I said for the umpteenth time. "My stomach's stuck to my backbone."

"Have a peanut-butter sandwich," Mum said, "but don't forget to clean up your mess."

"Oh, boy! Have we got peanut butter?"

"Yas." That's how Mum said yes when she was tickled about something. "I sold a bag of rags to the 'Addy-bone' man and I got enough money for a jar of peanut butter and a loaf of Dutch brown bread."

I stirred up the oil in the peanut-butter jar and slathered it on the bread. Mmmm, it smelled good. I had another slice and washed it all down with two cups of water. Then I forgot my mess and went to bed contented.

I fell asleep instantly and dreamed I owned a Custard Car. I drove it everywhere: to the store and to church and to Muskoka to show Aunt Aggie. I even let all the kids in the neighbourhood have a turn. All except Lorraine LaSquare, that is. Lorraine was the only kid on the street who owned a tricycle (her father had a job) and one day she said if all us poor kids would line up on the sidewalk she'd give us each a ride. Well, I was the last in line and when it came my turn she picked up her tricycle and went in to supper. I never got over that. So when it came her turn, in my dream, I picked up my Custard Car with superhuman strength and carried it into the house.

What a perfect dream to end a perfect day!

# 18

# S.W.A.K.

Dad and Arthur had gone up north at the beginning of the summer to help Grampa Thomson with the farm work. At first I was mad because I couldn't go. Uncle Charlie had taken them in his rumble seat and he said there wasn't room enough for me. But when I found out they wouldn't be back until school started again, I was glad I hadn't gone. The holidays seemed to last a lot longer when you stayed at home.

We had a nice time that summer. With Dad gone Mum had nobody to fight with, and with Arthur gone I had nobody to fight with. So the days stretched out in a long, peaceful, lazy-hazy string.

But before many weeks went by I began to miss Dad a lot, and one day I sat down and wrote him a big long letter. Willa made me an envelope and Mum gave me a two-cent stamp. I sealed the letter *S.W.A.K* and posted it on the way down Ellis Avenue.

Ellis Avenue was a long, gradual hill with Lake Ontario spread out at its foot like a huge blue swimming pool. I had never been in a real swimming pool myself, but I had seen two of them at a distance. One was the Mineral Baths on Bloor

Street, and the other was Sunnyside Bathing Pavilion.

The Mineral Baths were right opposite High Park. Willa said the twin pools used to be part of a hospital. At the Sunday School picnic all the kids lined up along the grassy banks and stared across Bloor Street at the lucky people diving from the tower and swishing down the slide into the gleaming mineral waters.

Sunnyside Bathing Pavilion was on the lakefront. We often strolled down the hot, treeless beach while our lunch was digesting and peered through the wire fence at the paying customers. I could never figure out why anybody would pay to swim in there when only a stone's throw away was glorious—free—Lake Ontario. Dad said they must have more money than brains. But Mum said she thought it would be lovely to bathe in that pretty turquoise-blue water.

The lake did have its drawbacks. Some days it was as cold and grey as a witch's heart (as Arthur would say) and other times the waves would come crashing, six feet high, over the breakwall.

But the worst thing that could possibly happen at the lake happened the day that I posted my letter to Dad. So I wrote him another one the very next day and told him all about it.

"Dear Dad." My neat writing that always amazed Willa was spoiled because my hand was shaking.

*You will be surprised to hear from me again so soon.*
*And you'll be surprised that Mum gave me another two-cent stamp, won't you? But when I tell you what happened yesterday, then you won't be surprised any more.*
*Remember I told you Willa was taking me swimming?*
*Well, she did but we didn't go in the water. I'll tell you*

why. Because there was an undertow and seven people got drowned, that's why. And one of the drowned people was someone we know. It was Lorraine LaSquare who lives next door to Hunter's grocery store. Do you know who I mean? She is that stingy girl who never gives me a ride on her bike. And now she can't ride it any more so ha! ha! (Mum just looked over my shoulder and said don't speak ill of the dead, so I won't.)

Do you want to know how come Willa and I got saved from drowning? I'll tell you how. It was all on account of the knots in my shoestrings. Lorraine LaSquare ran into the water hollering, 'Last one in's a rotten egg!' Then she disappeared. Well, by the time I got the knots undone and my shoes off everyone on the beach was yelling, 'Undertow! Undertow!' Willa and I just stood there staring at the spot where Lorraine went under, expecting her to pop up again. But she never did. Willa said that's one time it paid me to be sloppy, because Lorraine's shoes had been tied in nice neat bows. So I guess my sloppiness paid Willa too, because she had to wait for me.

Now I will tell you the best part. Do you know who is a hero and is going to get his picture in the paper and everything? Our cousin Buster, that's who. As you probably know, Buster is a strong swimmer, so he swam around on top of the water, grabbing people from underneath him and hauling them in to shore. He saved six people single-handed. Isn't that wonderful? But seven people got drowned, including my friend Lorraine LaSquare. Isn't that awful? I think I am going to be invited to her funeral. But Mum says the casket will probably be

*closed because Lorraine won't be fit to look at. Also Mum*
*says since I haven't got a black dress she'll have to dye my*
*old cotton playdress navy blue. Which, come to think of it,*
*might be an improvement.*

*All us kids have to stay in for three days and not play*
*any noisy games because Veeny Street is in mourning. All*
*the front-room blinds are pulled down. Even little kids like*
*Jakey can't go out and play tag because it is too noisy and*
*disrespectful. Willa said she'll get me a library book to keep*
*me occupied. She thinks I might like* Girl of the Limberlost.
*Ask Arthur has he ever read that book. Willa looked over*
*my shoulder and said don't be silly, it's a girls' book. But I*
*like lots of boys' books, so why wouldn't he like a girls'*
*book, I wonder.*

*Mum just came in from looking up the street and said the*
*wreath is on LaSquares' front door, so that means Lorraine*
*is home now. She said it is a pearl-grey wreath with a*
*pink bow on the bottom (because pink is for girls). I'm*
*going out to look.*

> *I hope you found this letter interesting,*
> *Your loving daughter,*
> *Bea.*

*P.S. Are you proud of me for saving Willa's life because*
*of the knots in my shoestrings? Mum says it had nothing*
*to do with shoestrings. It was God's will, she said. But I*
*don't know. What do you think, Dad?*

> *XXX OOO B.M.T.*

After the lake tragedy Mum wouldn't let us go swimming
any more. So I spent the rest of the summer playing street

games and baseball, and visiting people like Grampa and Maude and Billy Sundy.

Willa was too big to play street games, so when she wasn't busy helping Mum she went window shopping with her friends on Bloor Street. Once she and Evie walked all the way to Yonge and Bloor and Aunt Susan gave them each a box of nuts and a car ticket.

Street games were my favourite pastime. And there were lots of them to choose from—Oyster Sails and Red Light, Green Light and You Can't Cross The River. I liked Oyster Sails the best myself. ("Hoist Your Sails, not Oyster Sails," corrected Willa disdainfully. "Honestly, Bea, sometimes you're as dumb as a doornail.")

Oyster Sails was a twilight game. It never got underway until just before the streetlights came on and our mothers called us in. We'd choose sides, pick a leader and make up secret signals. Then off we'd go, hightailing it around the neighbourhood, the haunting cry of "Oyster Sails!" echoing eerily down darkening lanes and dusky streets and whispering alleyways.

We had a good Sunday School picnic that summer. It was held in High Park. I was hoping it would be at Centre Island because it's lots more fun going across the bay in a ferryboat than just walking along Bloor Street. But Mum said the Baptist church couldn't afford to go to the Island. Gladie said the Presbyterian picnic was going to be held there, so I decided next year I'd be a Presbyterian.

Right at the entrance to the park was a huge canvas sign stretched between two trees. On it in big black letters were the words *Gentiles Only*.

"What does it mean, Mum?" I was curious.

"It means no Jews allowed."

"What are we?" I asked anxiously.

"We're Gentiles," she said.

I was glad because if we were Jews we couldn't have our picnic in High Park.

I won an India-rubber ball in the races and ate fourteen salmon sandwiches for supper. So all in all I had a real good time.

I enjoyed my grown-up friends almost as much as friends my own age. I had lots of fun with Maude and Billy Sundy. Billy was very religious and every time he saw me he'd ask me if I was saved. I didn't have the least idea if I was or not but I always said yes anyway, just to hear him holler "Hallelujah."

Mrs. Sundy had nicknamed me Scallywag. One Saturday morning when I went over to their house she said to me, "Hello there, Scallywag. How would you like to help me with my cedar-mopping?" Of course I jumped at the chance and gave her back kitchen a real good cedar-mopping. Usually Mrs. Sundy just paid me with an apple or a cookie, but this time she handed me a nickel and said, "Away you go to the picture show." So I ran home as fast as my skinny legs would carry me to ask my mum if it was okay.

She was standing on tiptoe in front of the cracked kitchen mirror, plucking out white hairs from among the black ones.

"I earned a nickel from Mrs. Sundy, Mum," I burst out excitedly, "and she said I could go to the picture show. Can I, Mum, if I'm careful crossing Bloor Street?"

"Oh, I guess so, just so long as you don't talk to strangers," Mum said, plucking out a curly white strand. "And while you're up there go to the fifteen-cent store and get me some

Lovalon to cover up these unsightly white hairs. It looks as if I'm going to go prematurely grey, just like Puppa."

Lovalon Black Rinse was a packet of blue-black crystals that turned into hair dye when you dissolved it in hot water.

Mum went to the sideboard to get her purse, tut-tutting all the way about her grey hairs. But she couldn't find it. "My purse! My purse! I've lost my purse!" she cried, and raced upstairs in a panic.

Willa and I ran after her, searching in all the same places. "I don't know why she gets so upset about it," muttered my disgruntled sister, the dust rag still in her hand. "There's never anything in it anyway."

But that's the way Mum was. About twice a week she flew into a frenzy looking for her purse. And it always turned up in the most likely place. This time it was on top of the kitchen cabinet.

"I don't know who could have put it there," she remarked, rummaging breathlessly for the money.

"Will there be any change, Mum?" I asked hopefully, tying her nickel with mine in my hanky and shoving it down to the bottom of my pinny-pocket.

"No, Lovalon costs a nickel. And don't lose it. Money doesn't grow on trees, you know."

All the way to Bloor Street I daydreamed about a money tree in our backyard, just dripping with nickels and dimes. By the time I got to Kresge's, I had picked enough to buy myself a two-wheeler.

I got to the Lyndhurst just in time to buy my ticket and find a seat in the front row. Then the lights dimmed and the curtains parted and the audience erupted in a wild, deafening roar. I held my ears and stamped my feet and hollered with the rest. It's a wonder the roof didn't come tumbling down.

Unlike those of the Kingswood Theatre in Birchcliff, all the picture shows at the Lyndhurst were talkies. This one was about a police dog called Rin Tin Tin. He was a terrific dog, that Rinny. He understood English like a person. And brave. He went through fires and floods and snowstorms, catching all the bad guys and saving all the good guys. Then after that came a cowboy serial starring Ken Maynard and his horse. It was the most exciting thing I had ever seen. But just as the horse and my cowboy hero jumped off the cliff into the cloudless sky the screen went black and a sign flashed on saying *Continued next week*. Try as I might, I couldn't get another nickel, so I never did find out what happened.

Dad and Arthur came home at the end of August. I was sprawled on Grampa Cole's front lawn chewing grass roots when I saw them trudging up Windermere Avenue, bent over double with sacks on their backs. I ran to meet them hollering, "Addybones!" That started a fight with Arthur right away so we got back to normal in no time.

The second they set foot in the kitchen, Mum said, "You two will need a bath before you sit down to the table."

"Ya, Arthur, you smell like panure!" I taunted.

"Ba-nure, dumb-bell! " he retorted.

"Ma-nure, dopey," corrected Willa, keeping her distance.

The stewing meat had been simmering all day long and by suppertime it was as tender as fresh bread. Mum cooked some new potatoes (from the sacks on Dad's and Arthur's backs) with some baby carrots from our own back garden. When they were done, crisp tender, she drained them both into a pint sealer so as not to throw the goodness down the sink. Then she used the vegetable water to make the rich brown gravy, and dumped the whole works into the big mixing bowl. Ahhh, heavenly stew! And to top it off she had made a rhubarb custard pie (rhuberb, Mum called it) from Gladie's mother's garden. Dad said the way his kids ate he'd swear we all had hollow legs. And for once he patted his own lean stomach and declared he was full to the brim.

After supper he gave Jakey and me a big brown copper and Willa a whole nickel. Then he went straight over to Billy and Maude Sundy's. When he came back he announced proudly that the rent was all caught up.

Just before I fell asleep that night I heard my parents' voices sifting up through the dining room stovepipe hole. (The stove had been taken down for the summer and the hole was covered by a tin plate with a pretty mountain picture on it.)

I couldn't hear what they were saying, but I could tell by the soft tone of their voices that there wasn't going to be a fight that night.

# 19

# Kids' day at the Ex

Mum was busy as a beaver getting our clothes ready for school. Every stitch we wore had to be turned up or let down, and washed and ironed and mended. Mum could darn a hole or sew a patch that absolutely could not be seen by the naked eye.

It was her way of making up for the things we lacked. She believed, almost religiously, that if we looked "clean and paid for" our teachers would know that we came from a good home and would treat us accordingly. She was only partly right. We did get more respect than the poor shabby kids whose clothes were held together with safety pins, but we ranked well below the ones who looked as if they had just stepped out from the pages of Eaton's Spring and Summer Catalogue.

I dreaded the first day of school. To me it was like the start of a ten month jail sentence. The only thing that made it bearable was that it coincided with the coming of the 'Ex.' The Canadian National Exhibition was the biggest annual exposition in the world. And it was ours!

On the last day of the school year every Ontario youngster

got a free pass for kids' day at the Ex. All summer long I worried that my free pass might somehow disappear out of the sideboard drawer and I'd be the only kid in Toronto who didn't get to go. Mum had to show it to me at least a hundred times over the summer to reassure me.

Then the day before kids' day I was overcome with another big worry. I was petrified I'd sleep in the next morning and miss our free ride. So I decided to run over to Gladie's house and make her promise not to go without me.

I waited at the curb for the Canada Bread wagon to pass by. "Hi, Bessie!" I called out gaily to the familiar old brown mare. Bessie snorted and Andy, the baker, waved a greeting with his whip. From underneath the wagon I could see two feet dangling down. As it passed by, I saw that the feet belonged to Arthur. He was sitting on the step where the baker rests his basket, enjoying a free ride.

"Hookey on behind!" I squealed triumphantly.

Andy yanked on the reins and poor old Bessie stumbled to a stop. Off tumbled Arthur and away I ran, with him in hot pursuit. Gladie saw me coming and flung open the door. I streaked inside like greased lightning and just managed to slam the door in my brother's furious face.

Laughing hysterically, Gladie and I watched through the door curtains as the baker collared Arthur. Waving the whip threateningly, he gave Arthur a good tongue-lashing for hookeying on behind.

Gladie thought up a swell plan so I wouldn't sleep in the next day. "We'll make a long string," she said, and you can tie it to your toe and throw it out your bedroom window. Then I'll come over and yank it in the morning." So we knotted a hundred bits of string together and she promised, cross her heart, not to forget to yank it.

I was scared to go home for supper because I knew Arthur would be out to get me. Of course, he would have done the same thing in my place. Hollering "hookey on behind" was a neighbourhood tradition. But lucky for me I saw Willa coming down the street so I followed her in and Arthur didn't dare touch me because she was still bigger than he was.

Next morning, bright and early, Gladie ran over and pulled the string. And so did all the other kids on the street. By seven-thirty we were all bouncing merrily along Lakeshore Road in the back of Sandy Beasley's rattly old slat-sided truck. The lake rippled like a pan of gold in the sunrise. A cool wind blew across it, standing our hair on end. We looked like a bunch of dandelions gone to seed.

"*One, two, three, four, who are we for?*" sang out Buster lustily.

"*Swansea! Swansea! Rah! Rah! Rah!*" we answered.

Swansea was a separate village in those days and most of us kids were proud descendants of its earliest settlers. (Veeny Street was named after my great-aunt Veeny who was Grampa Cole's dead sister.)

We arrived at the Dufferin Gates a whole hour before they opened, so we had to sit on the curb and wait.

"I hope I don't get turned away," worried big tall Minnie Beasley. "I got no carfare home. I got to wait for Uncle Sandy."

Poor Minnie. Her parents had died suddenly of galloping consumption and she had to live with her aunt and uncle and help take care of their ten children. Mum said it was a shame the way they 'bused her.

Someone had given her a kid's ticket, but she wasn't a kid any more. She was eighteen and hadn't been to school for years.

"Let your hair down, Minnie. That'll make you look younger," suggested Willa.

Minnie unfastened her old-fashioned bun and shook a cascade of red ringlets down her back.

"Take your shoes off so you'll be shorter," I said.

"Stoop down and we'll all go through in a bunch, with you in the middle," was Buster's helpful suggestion.

It was exciting, thinking of ways to make sure Minnie didn't get turned away. It made the time go faster. Not one of us had a watch so we had no idea when the hour was up.

Our plan worked like a charm. We all surged in together and nobody questioned Minnie's ticket.

At the fountain, after deciding what time to meet to go home, we broke up into families. Grampa had given each of us a quarter. It was the most money I'd ever had in my life and I couldn't wait to spend it. The first thing I wanted to buy was a gas balloon. But Willa wouldn't let me. She pried open my fingers, took the quarter and snapped it into her change purse. "If you spend it now you won't have anything to look forward to all day long," she reminded me sternly. I knew she was right, but I could hardly bear to part with it.

Arthur and I always buried the hatchet on Kids' Day, no matter what. He was still mad at me for snitching to the baker, but he held my hand when Willa told him to. "We don't want to get separated and have to waste the whole day looking for each other," she said wisely.

We did the rounds of the buildings in the morning. Willa's

favourite was the Flower Building, so we went there first. Arthur's was the Manufacturer's Building so we went there next. Mine was the Horse Palace and we went there last. Willa said, "Pewww!" and held her nose the whole time we were in there.

Then we headed for the Pure Food Building to line up for free samples. At least, Arthur and I lined up. Willa spent her time entering contests. She must have filled out a hundred entry blanks. *Win a bicycle! Win a car! Win a year's supply of groceries!* Who could believe it? It seemed like a terrible waste of time to me, and she hardly got any free samples.

Arthur and I kept running back to the end of the line to get more. By the time noonhour came we were absolutely stuffed with pork and beans, soup, bologna, pickles, cheese and crackers, and I can't remember what all. We were so full we could hardly eat our cucumber sandwiches, so we saved the leftovers for supper.

The Grandstand Show took up most of the afternoon. We got in free with our Kids' Day ticket. We went in early and got wonderful seats right in the middle of the huge curved stand.

It was such a long wait in the boiling sun that Arthur finally said, "Let's go. I'm sick of waiting." And I said "Yeah, and gimme my quarter. I wanna buy some pop and a red-hot."

"Shut up, both of you," barked Willa. "It'll be starting any minute now and it'll be worth the wait. You'll see. And I'm not missing a free show just because you two have ants in your pants."

Arthur and I nearly died laughing at our prim sister saying such a thing. And she was right, as usual. It was the most glorious show in the whole world. There were acrobats and

143

trapeze artists, animal acts and magicians, and a man was even shot out of a cannon before our very eyes and lived to tell the tale. Then, at the end of the whole wonderful performance, came the musical ride of the Royal Canadian Mounted Police in their beautiful scarlet uniforms.

The sun was leaning far to the west by the time we got to the midway. We had no money to spend on rides, so we pressed right on through the crowd to the sideshows.

A barker stood on a wooden platform yelling through a makeshift megaphone. "Step right up, folks . . . Step inside. Only twenty-five cents, a quarter of a dollar, to view all the wonders of the world!"

A huge tent billowed mysteriously behind him. Overhead flapped gaudy pictures of the hidden wonders: a two-headed baby grinned impishly from both its dimpled mouths; a bearded lady twirled her spiky, waxed mustache; and the India Rubber Man tied himself in knots beside an ugly dog-faced boy.

"Willa, Willa, give me my quarter!" I cried beseechingly.

"Don't be silly. It's a waste of money," she snapped.

"Aren't they real?" I asked, wanting desperately to believe.

"No. Only the midgets are real."

As if to prove her right, at that very moment a little tiny lady was being lifted to the stand by a great big man who leapt nimbly up beside her.

"Ladies and gentlemen, your attention please!" cried the barker, and the crowd quieted obediently. "You see before you the world's most unique mother and son. The son weighs in at two hundred pounds, the little mother at thirty-six and a half. At birth this young man was one quarter of his mother's weight. If you don't believe me, ask them for yourself."

"That's disgusting," sniffed a lady behind me.

"There's a family resemblance," said her companion.

"Hey there, fella, that really your mother?" asked a nervy red-nosed man.

"I swear by all that's holy," declared the two-hundred pounder, holding up a Bible. "If I'm lying, may God strike me dead!"

The crowd glanced furtively heavenward, but nothing happened.

"Do you believe him, Willa?" asked Arthur.

"Noooo," answered Willa uncertainly.

Well, I believed him. Who but a fool or a madman would tell a big fat lie with a Bible in his hand?

After covering every inch of the midway we headed, footsore and weary, to the lakefront. Dropping down on the littered, matted brown grass, we finished up our lunch. Above us the azure sky was gaily polka-dotted with escaping gas balloons. I was glad Willa hadn't let me buy one.

"See that long cloud up there shaped like a big cigar?" said Arthur, munching on a soggy sandwich.

"Don't talk while you're eating," Willa said.

"It looks like the R–100," Arthur said, ignoring her.

"What's an R–100?" I asked, leaning back on my elbows to watch gas balloons go drifting through the cloud.

"It's a dirigible. An airship. It sailed over Toronto a couple of years ago."

"How come I didn't see it?"

"It was real early in the morning."

"How come you saw it then?"

"Because I was going to the bathroom, stupid."

"Let's go," said Willa. "It's getting late."

"I have to put Sloane's Liniment on first," said Arthur, pulling the bottle of amber liquid out of his knickers pocket. "My growing pains are killing me."

Arthur never went to the Ex without his liniment. After giving his knees a treatment, he handed the bottle to me. "Peww!" said Willa, but she rubbed a little on her knees too. The stinging liniment felt good, soaking into our aching joints and easing the pain away.

Our second visit to the Pure Food Building was our last stop. Finally Willa relinquished our quarters. Then came the big decision. Back and forth we went from booth to booth trying to decide what to buy. Willa settled on a Neilson's bag and I followed suit. In it were six nickel chocolate bars, a pink blotter for school, a cardboard hat to wear home on the streetcar so everyone would know where we'd been, a sausage-shaped balloon and a miniature can of Neilson's cocoa. Arthur spent his quarter on a Rowntree's bag just to be different. But the contents were exactly the same except our hats were shaped like a crown and his had a peak on it.

"Mine's better," I said.

"Mine is!" he retorted.

"It's six of one and half a dozen of the other," remarked our sister dryly.

Dusk was falling. One by one the coloured lights blinked on as we made our weary way to the fountain. The gang gathered, a few at a time. We were too tired to talk, so we just gazed up at the pretty rainbows the fountain was spraying into the navy blue sky.

Sandy Beasley's truck was waiting for us at the gates. Scrambling over the wobbly sides, we huddled together on the splintery floor. The air seemed suddenly chilly as the truck lumbered away from the star-spangled world of the exhibition grounds.

Minnie Beasley started chanting, "*Ice cream, soda water, ginger ale and pop. Swansea, Swansea is always on the top!*" But nobody could be bothered joining in.

Limping through the backyard of our stuck-together house, we smelled the spicy, mouth-watering aroma of simmering chili sauce escaping from the open kitchen door. While the chili sauce was evaporating to just the right thickness, Mum was busy darning a sock stretched over a burnt-out light bulb. On the cutting board on the table, Dad was carving out a piece of rubber tire to fit the heel of his boot.

Proudly, each of us presented our mother with our miniature cans of cocoa. "Glory be!" she exclaimed appreciatively. "I'll be able to make a thumping big chocolate cake with all that lovely cocoa."

Dad put aside his work and blew up our balloons.

"Jakey can have mine," Willa said.

"Billy can have mine," Arthur said.

I kept mine and it didn't break for a week. Boy, was I glad I'd let Willa take charge of my quarter!

# 20
# "Happy Birthday, Booky"

Aunt Milly invited us all up for supper on Billy's and my birthday. It was a rare treat to be asked to somebody's house for a meal during the Depression. It probably used up Aunt Milly's whole week's food voucher to feed the bunch of us. But that's the way she was, Aunt Milly. She always said the more you give away, the more that comes back to you.

Things weren't going too well at home. Mum and Dad were still fighting all the time; the rent was overdue again; there wasn't a speck of coal in the dugout; and the kitchen cabinet was nearly as bare as Mother Hubbard's cupboard. Then, like a ray of sunshine on a cloudy day, came the invitation.

Aunt Milly and Uncle Mort lived on Durie Street, just below Bloor. About four in the afternoon we started walking over. I walked ahead, pushing the baby in the old reed sulky. One of the wheels was bent, and it was hard to push. It went *thump, thump, thump* along the sidewalk, making Billy laugh. He had on a blue knitted outfit Mum had made from an unravelled sweater. The colour matched his eyes exactly. He was cute as a button when he wasn't crying. It was hard to believe he was the same pitiful baby born just a year ago that day.

Aunt Milly and Uncle Mort had three children. The youngest was a darling baby girl about Billy's age. She was named Bonny because she was so pretty. The middle child was a boy called Sunny because he was sunny-natured. The oldest was a girl called Dimples, and every time she smiled you could tell the reason why. Of course, these weren't their real names. They were just nicknames Aunt Milly had made up. I asked her once what nickname she would give me if I were her little girl. "Bunny," she answered promptly, "because you're quick as a rabbit and cute as a bunny." I liked that.

Aunt Milly's suppers were always something special. You never knew what to expect. So we could hardly wait to get there to find out what was in store for us.

"Halloo, dears!" came her gay greeting at the door. Uncle Mort hung our coats on the hallway hooks and we all trooped down the hall to the kitchen.

A coal fire crackled in the kitchen stove, making it warm and cosy. We hadn't had a fire in our stove yet, even though it was the beginning of November.

In her cute yellow housedress, with her auburn curls bouncing on her girlish shoulders, Aunt Milly flitted about the kitchen like a canary in a Hawthorne bush.

"What can I do for you, Milly?" Mum asked.

"You can sit yourself down, that's what," returned her younger sister. "Arthur and Willa will help me, won't you, kidlets?" She gave them a wink through thick mascara-darkened lashes.

She didn't have to ask twice. They both jumped up eagerly and ran to do her bidding.

Uncle Mort was as handsome as his wife was pretty. And he

was nice too. He offered Dad his tobacco pouch the minute they sat down, and told him to roll his own. Dad liked that.

Sunny and Dimples took Jakey down the cellar to play, and I squatted on the floor to amuse the babies. Bonny was walking already. Back and forth she toddled bringing toys to Billy. He sat on a pink blanket, his long legs spread-eagled to give him balance. He hadn't even stood up yet, let alone walked. So Bonny seemed awfully smart by comparison. Until she started to talk. That's when she had to take a back seat to our Billy. Her baby-chatter sounded like pure gibberish compared to his clear words and bright little sentences.

"I never heard anything like it, Franny," marvelled Aunt Milly. "It's uncanny, a baby talking before he can walk. Why, he's as sharp as a tack."

Mum and I exchanged proud glances.

It was lovely to see everybody happy and having a good time—Dad talking and smoking, instead of yelling; Mum smiling and relaxing, instead of nagging. It just did my heart good.

"Soup's on!" cried Aunt Milly, waving us to the table with her long red fingernails.

Uncle Mort held Bonny on his lap so Billy could use her high chair. Arthur and Willa sat on either side of Aunt Milly and I got squeezed on a kitchen stool between Mum and Dad. The three little ones sat like a row of midgets on the wash bench behind the table.

When dinner was served, it wasn't soup at all—it was fish and chips and ketchup! And instead of tea or cocoa or water to wash it down with, we each got a green glass bottle of Coca-Cola. One at every place!

"You shouldn't waste your money on soft drinks for us,

Milly," Mum said, taking a big slurp that started her hiccupping.

"It sure is fizzy stuff," Dad laughed. "It went right up my nose."

It tasted so good I could hardly believe it. Even better than Vernor's ginger ale at Eaton's. I wanted to sip it slowly the way Willa and Arthur had the sense to do, but a sudden craving came over me and I slopped the whole works down in five seconds flat.

"I've still got half mine left," teased Arthur.

"You should have made it last, Bea," chided Willa.

"Don't make a pig of yourself," scolded Dad.

My eyes brimmed with tears, but Mum stemmed the flood with her yearly warning. "If you cry on your birthday, Bea, it means you'll cry all the year round."

Then Aunt Milly came to my rescue. "Fiddle dee dee," she said, "there's more where that came from." She disappeared into the cellarway and came back with another whole carton. Boy, did Willa and Arthur empty their bottles in a hurry!

I made sure my second Coke lasted until all my fish and chips were gone. The mixture of those delicious flavours, all going down together, was just too wonderful to describe.

Mum jumped up to help clear the table.

"No you don't, Fran. You just sit back and relax. You look all fagged out."

"Thank you, Milly," sighed Mum, settling back gratefully.

Poor Mum. We hardly ever paid attention to how tired she was.

When the table was cleared, Aunt Milly disappeared again, this time into the pantry. Out she came carrying a lighted birthday cake, and everyone joined in singing "Happy Birthday" to Billy and me. Eleven pink candles encircled the round chocolate cake, with a blue one in the middle for Billy.

Uncle Mort switched off the kitchen light. I'll never forget that moment—that magical moment of flickering lights and glowing faces and shadows bouncing on the walls.

"Lights! Lights!" cried Billy, gleefully clapping his hands, the yellow flames dancing in his eyes.

I showed him how to make an "O" with his mouth and we huffed and puffed and blew the candles out together.

"Did you make a wish, Bea?" asked Willa.

"Oh, darn! I forgot!" I cried worriedly.

"It's too late now!" jeered Arthur.

"Indeed it's not," retorted Aunt Milly, handing me the bread knife. "You can wish while you're making the first cut, Bea. That works every time."

I made my usual wish, that I'd pass the following June, and hoped with all my might that Aunt Milly knew what she was talking about.

Uncle Mort began putting Dixie cups of ice cream and little wooden spoons in front of us.

"My stars, Milly," Mum exclaimed, her curiosity getting the better of her. "How in the world do you do it? How on earth can you afford all these treats? I haven't had ice cream and soft drinks in a month of Sundays."

"Fair trade's no robbery, Fran," asserted Aunt Milly, raising her plucked eyebrows. "I just ask the grocer for ice cream and Coke and he writes down peas and potatoes. What does he care? It's all the same as long as he gets paid."

"But—but—" spluttered Mum, "you're not allowed to get

confections on your relief voucher, Milly. You could get in trouble."

"That's why he puts down potatoes and peas. Try it, Fran. It's easy."

"I'd never get away with it," Mum said, a bit miffed. "I haven't got your way with people, Milly."

"We haven't even got a lump of coal, never mind ice cream and soft drinks," put in Dad sullenly.

"Coal?" chirped Aunt Milly mischievously. "You need coal? Run down the cellar and get Jim a bag of coal, Morty. Share and share alike, that's my motto."

Mum shook her head in disbelief. What would her outrageous little sister think of next?

When the dishes were done (I didn't have to help because it was my birthday) there were presents for the baby and me. I got brown ribbed stockings and flannelette bloomers, and a Big Little Book from Aunt Milly. Billy got Doctor Denton Sleepers and a rubber duck. It was a terrific birthday party, the best I'd ever had.

We started off home under a cold night sky. "Love you!" Aunt Milly called after us.

Mum pushed the sulky with the bag of coal hidden under Billy's covers. "Might as well keep it under wraps," her sister had said. "If you get asked no questions, you can tell no lies."

Dad carried Billy inside his khaki coat with only his head poking out. "Lights! Lights!" cried the baby, his head flung back, staring up at the starry sky.

We hurried home and rushed inside to get warm. But the kitchen was as cold as stone. Right away Dad stuffed the stove with torn paper and broken sticks and set a match to them. In seconds the fire roared up the chimney. Then, lump by lump, he added the precious fuel and put what was left in the coal shuttle.

Mum closed the door between the dining room and kitchen and soon it was warm and cosy. We undressed by the stove, being careful not to look at one another. Mum heated up the iron to make warm spots on our sheets.

"Happy Birthday, Booky," she said as she kissed my forehead and tucked the thin covers under my chin.

Booky. It was a nice nickname. I liked it even better than Bunny. And a lot better than Scatterbrain.

# 21

# Turkey and mistletoe

The Christmas season started out a lot better than it had the year before. Dad got a few weeks' work shovelling snow, Aunt Aggie sent us a chicken again and two Swansea churches gave us food hampers. Mum hadn't decided which one to belong to yet, the Presbyterian or the Baptist, so we shilly-shallied back and forth between them, and that's how come we got two hampers. And besides that there were Star Boxes too!

Stuffing was piled high in the mixing bowl on the shelf of the kitchen cabinet. Christmas cake was aging in a tin on the sideboard, and plum pudding sat on a plate wrapped in cheesecloth ready for steaming. Mum had made them both way back in November.

On Christmas Eve Dad strung the red and green crepe paper streamers from corner to corner of the dining room. In the middle, where they came together, he hung the red paper fold-out bell. It was beautiful!

Then after supper he went out to get the tree. Jakey and I stationed ourselves at the front room window to wait for him. It wasn't long before we saw him humping down the street, his left shoulder riding up and down with his short left leg, a snowy spruce tree sweeping a wide path behind him.

He made a sturdy stand out of two pieces of crossed wood and nailed it to the bottom of the tree. Dragging it through the dining room, he set it up in the front room corner. It was the biggest tree we'd ever had. Its tip touched the ten-foot ceiling.

"Let's go to bed, Bea-Bea," begged Jakey, his brown eyes glistening.

"Okay," I agreed, even though it was only seven o'clock and I wasn't the least bit tired.

Snuggling under the covers with Dad's greatcoat piled on top, I began the ritual of the Christmas stories. The old beliefs came flooding back with the telling. I decided to give Santa one more chance.

The next morning our stockings were filled with the usual stuff—an apple, an orange and some candy cushions. But at the foot of the bed were two wonderful surprises—a bright red fire engine for Jakey and a green and red telephone for me. The very one I had asked for last year. Squealing with delight, we hightailed it down the hall to show our parents what Santa had brought.

All morning long Jakey shrilled his fire engine around the bare wood floor in front of the Christmas tree and I telephoned everybody under the sun. Arthur said the screeching siren and jangling bells would drive a man to drink. Then he took a long swig out of a gingerbeer bottle full of water. But he wasn't really mad, because he was too busy enjoying his new art pad and box of paints. Willa had put on her Sunday dress to show off her pink pearl beads. And Billy was chewing happily on the soft brown ear of his brand-new teddy bear.

Halfway through the morning, Dad stepped outside to put some garbage in the tin. Then he stepped back in again with a puzzled expression on his face. He had a bulky brown parcel in one hand and a sheaf of long white envelopes in the other.

"I found these on top of the garbage lid," he said, setting the brown parcel on the table.

A name was scrawled across each envelope—*Willa, Arthur, Beatrice, John* and *William*. Dad scratched his head and handed them around to us.

Eagerly we tore them open to find a beautiful Christmas card inside with a quarter taped to each. But no signature.

"Who could have done it?" wondered our bewildered Dad.

"I know! I know!" I screeched, renewed faith breaking over me. "Santa! To make up for last year!"

"He doesn't give money, dumb-bell!" scoffed Arthur. (But I noticed he didn't say there was no Santa Claus.)

"Oh, mercy, my fingers are all thumbs," Mum said struggling with the parcel. Then she gasped as she lifted a big fat fowl from the wrappings.

"That's a whopper of a chicken," Dad said.

"It's not a chicken, it's a turkey," Willa said.

"And it's all cleaned, ready for the oven," Mum marvelled, bending down to inspect the dark interior. A turkey! Imagine! With drumsticks as big as my fist!

Dad was studying the envelope the baby's card had come in. "The handwriting looks familiar," he mused.

Mum studied it too. Then she jumped up on the little stool that made her tall enough to reach the top of the kitchen cabinet and jumped down again with the "Neilson's Chocolates" receipt box in her hand. Rummaging through it, she found last month's rent receipt and held it out beside the envelope.

"'William' is written exactly the same as Billy Sundy's signature," Dad said.

"Didn't I tell you it was our lucky day when we moved into Billy and Maude's house?" Mum cried, tee-heeing and rubbing her hands in that excited way she had.

Dad just shook his head. He could hardly credit a landlord who gave his tenants food and gifts instead of sending the bailiff around to put them out.

"What'll we do with Aunt Aggie's chicken?" asked Arthur.

"It'll keep," Mum said. "I'll tie it in a potato sack and hang it out on the line. It'll freeze solid in no time and be fresh as a daisy for New Year's. Maybe we'll ask Charlie and Myrtle and little Sarah over to share it with us. Except Charlie spoils that baby so badly I can hardly bear the little imp."

In the afternoon I ran over to Grampa's. Joey was perched on the stool, nibbling. He fixed me with the evil eye.

"Where's Grampa?" I asked nervously.

"Who wants to know?" he growled.

Lucky for me I didn't have to answer because just then Grampa came up from the cellar. "Hello there, Be-*a*-trice." His mouth curved under his moustache. "Was Santa good to you this year?"

I showed him my toy telephone and told him all about what everybody got, and about the mysterious stuff on top of the garbage lid. While I talked, a mile a minute, he lifted a huge golden goose from the wood-stove oven. Mum had asked them over to our house, but Grampa had said no, she had enough mouths to feed.

He didn't have a Christmas box for me and I didn't expect

one. I knew he had too many grandchildren to buy presents for. But he had something for me just the same. With a quick twist of his wiry wrist, he snapped the drumstick off the golden goose and dropped it in a bag.

"Are you givin' *her* the leg of our goose, Pa?" cried Joey angrily.

His father didn't answer. Instead he ripped off the other leg, clean as a whistle, and dropped it in beside its greasy mate.

"Merry Christmas, Be-*a*-trice," he said, handing me the steaming hot bag.

I didn't dare look at Joey. I just took the aromatic present, kissed my Grampa under his moustache and high-tailed it home through the lane.

I steered clear of Grampa's for weeks after that. Finally he came over to see if I was sick.

"I got worried, Be-*a*-trice," he said.

"I'm sorry, Grampa," I said. "But I'm scared of Joey. He always gives me dirty looks, and he never smiles even when I smile first."

My words made his eyes cloud over. "You mustn't pay him any mind." There was a catch in his voice. "His bark is worse than his bite. You got to remember that he was younger than you when he lost his ma. I'm all he's got left."

That's when I understood how it was with Joey. And Evie too. I couldn't imagine what it would be like to have no mother. No Mum to iron my bed in winter; no Mum to take me downtown to Eaton's; no Mum to call me Booky. I'd be jealous too, if Dad was all I had left.

After that I managed to conquer my fear of my boy-uncle, and many's the laugh we had, when we grew up, about him sitting in the corner chewing seeds and spitting husks and growling like a bear to scare me off.

That Christmas night I went to bed contented, but I was so elated I couldn't fall asleep. Willa was sawing it off beside me and the boys had long since settled down. Even Billy. Come to think of it, he seemed to sleep a lot sounder now that his cot was in the boys' room.

The warm, happy day kept going through my mind like a talking-picture show. Mum and Dad hadn't had a crabby word between them. I had spent the whole peaceful day talking on my telephone and reading a book Willa had given me called *Anne of Green Gables*. I loved every word of it. Then and there I decided to be a writer when I grew up.

As I read, I gnawed away on one of my goose legs. The minute Arthur saw it he hollered, "Bits on you!" and Mum made me give him and Jakey the other leg to share. Lucky for me, Willa hated goose. "Eww!" she cried, wrinkling her nose. "I wouldn't touch the greasy thing with a ten-foot pole!" When the meat was gone I sucked the bone for hours. By the time I threw it in the garbage tin it was as clean and bare as a clothes pin.

Then came the turkey dinner. Instead of a drumstick, Dad gave me a slice of breast for a change. I'd never tasted anything like it, so succulent and tender. The rest of my plate overflowed with fluffy mashed potatoes, spicy bread dressing and lots of bright-coloured vegetables all glistening with golden brown gravy.

"Save room for plum pudding!" Mum cried. As if we needed reminding.

Then after the pudding came Christmas cake! "It would kill

a man twice to eat one slice of Mrs. Thomson's Christmas cake!" sang Mum gaily as she sliced up the delicious dark fruit loaf.

Thinking about all that lovely food made me hungry again. So I got up out of bed and tiptoed down the stairs. Only the kitchen light was on, so I saw them but they didn't see me.

Willa had tied a sprig of mistletoe to the light chain and Mum and Dad were kissing under it! My heart skipped a beat and thrills ran up my spine. What a way to finish Christmas!

I crept back up the stairs again and they never knew I was there.

# 22

# Incredible news

My hollow tooth was acting up again. Every night Mum had to stuff it full of cotton soaked in oil of cloves. But that didn't help much. So one cold February day Dad took me downtown to the Dental College to have it pulled.

Boy, was that awful! The student dentist was young and smart-alecky, and he snickered at me the whole time he was doing it. Then, after he'd nearly killed me, Dad paid with a quarter and we left.

On the Dundas streetcar Dad handed me his clean hanky to hold against my mouth. Then he opened the window a crack so I wouldn't get sick. A nice lady across the aisle gave me a pitying look as the hanky slowly turned wet and crimson.

A warm sweet smell drifted in the open window.

"I smell hot cocoa, Dad," I mumbled through the soggy hanky.

"That would be Neilson's Chocolate Factory," Dad said. "You can smell it for miles around."

"Can we stop and ask for free bits, Dad?" (I had heard, through the grapevine, that Neilson's gave away free chocolate bits, the way Canada Bread sometimes gave away broken biscuits.)

"If we get off we'll have to walk the rest of the way," Dad said, looking at me anxiously. "Are you sure you're up to it?"

"I'm sure," I said, wiping the pink dribble off my chin and longing for the chocolate in spite of my sore mouth. "Please, Dad!"

The lady smiled encouragement. Dad smiled back and we jumped off the streetcar at the next stop. Neilson's was only a hop, skip and jump up Gladstone Avenue.

Just as we approached the factory, two men came staggering down the front steps carrying a stretcher. Over it was thrown a lumpy grey blanket with a pair of big black boots sticking out. The soles of the boots were covered with dark, thick chocolate.

Hastily Dad removed his cap and laid it flat against his chest. Respectfully I hung my head as the stretcher passed by and was loaded into a waiting ambulance.

It had no sooner pulled away from the curb than a man at the factory door said to Dad, "You looking for work, Mister?"

"Yes, sir!" answered Dad, clicking his heels like a soldier.

"Well, I just lost my maintenance man." The man jerked his head in the direction of the disappearing ambulance. "The job's yours if you can start first thing in the morning. Hours are eight to six, six days a week. Pay's twelve dollars. If you'll follow me, I'll sign you up and give you a week's advance."

My legs started to shake with excitement, so I sat down on a green bench in the entranceway while Dad went into the office. Was it really happening? Could it be true? When Dad came out, his face beaming, I knew it was.

"Would you like a bag of chocolate bits to take home with you, Missy?" asked Dad's new boss kindly.

"Yes, please," I whispered, my heart in my mouth.

We practically ran all the way home with our wonderful, glorious news.

It was Monday, so it was washday. The kitchen was draped from corner to corner with frozen flannelette sheets. They smelled clean and frosty, and they crackled when you brushed against them. It was like walking into an icy white maze. We couldn't tell who was in the kitchen.

"Don't lay a finger on my clean sheets!" Mum barked, tired and crabby, as usual, from scrubbing on the board all day. So we ducked under, and it was then she saw the smile on Dad's face.

"What are you grinning about?" she snapped crankily.

"I've got a job!" The words flew from his lips like a bird let loose from its cage. He could no more hold them back than I could still the wild beating of my heart.

"An odd job?" Mum asked, too quickly.

"No," Dad cried indignantly, "a full-time job. A steady, paying job! I've got work!"

"Steady—full-time—work!" repeated Mum dazedly.

The incredible news brought everybody out of hiding. Jakey popped up from under the table. Willa sidled through the sheets from the direction of the sink. Arthur appeared out of nowhere, and the baby started to cry for attention from the high chair. Dad scooped him up and tossed him in the air and the crying changed to gurgling, bubbling laughter. Nobody spoke. They just stood there gaping as if they daren't believe their ears. Then Dad told them the whole story.

"It was all Bea's doing," he said, smiling down at me and giving my head a pat. "If she hadn't persuaded me to stop, in spite of her sore jaw and against my better judgement, I never would have landed that job." Boy, was I proud of myself. And of my Dad, the maintenance man!

Willa and Arthur both gave me admiring glances. So I dumped my chocolate bits out on the table and told them to help themselves.

\* \* \*

Dad was never out of work again. The humiliations of the pogey and the bread lines, the Star Boxes and the food hampers were all behind him now. He even allowed himself an occasional luxury, like a nickel packet of Sweet Caps or a package of "roll-your-owns."

And Mum finally got her washing-machine. A Thor, just like Aunt Hester's. She joined the Home Lover's Club at Eaton's and paid for it at two dollars a month, so it never had to go back to the store. And she kept her vow about the Annex too. It never saw her again for dust!

# About the Author

Bernice Thurman Hunter was a storyteller from an early age. When her own children were small, she wrote stories for them, but it was not until they were grown up that she began to get her work published. Soon she had become one of Canada's favourite writers of historical fiction, with a dozen books to her credit, including the Booky and Margaret trilogies, *Lamplighter, The Railroader, Amy's Promise* and *Janey's Choice.*

Many of Bernice's books were based on her own childhood and family, bringing Canada's history to vivid life for readers of all ages and making Booky one of Canada's most memorable characters, not only in the best-selling trilogy of books but also in a stage play, a musical, and a series of television movies.

Her books also received much critical acclaim. *With Love From Booky* was shortlisted for the Ruth Schwartz Award, *That Scatterbrain Booky* won the IODE Award and was runner-up for the City of Toronto Book Award, and *Amy's Promise* won the Red Cedar Award. Bernice herself was honoured with the Vicky Metcalf Award for her contribution to Canadian children's literature, and was a member of the Order of Canada. She died in 2002.

# Other books by
# Bernice Thurman Hunter: